Brave Horse

Praise for the Mustang Mountain Series

I love your Mustang Mountain books! I have the entire series of them. When I would start to read one I couldn't put it down. What awesome stories...
                                    Skye

...You're a great author and I love all of your books. I myself have always wanted a paint/pinto and when I saw the picture of the wild horse Shadow I knew I would want to read it.
                                    Jamie

I absolutely loved your books Sky Horse, Fire Horse *and* Night Horse. *My favorite book was* Night Horse. *I liked this book because of how all the characters changed.*
                                    Kaila

I love your books so much they are my favorite books of all time and I encourage you to write more books about horses because I an a HORSE FANATIC!!!!!
                                    Josh

Hey, I am a 14-year-old girl from Norway. I love your books so much that I read them over and over!
                                    Malene

(Sharon writes back to all the fans who write to her at her email address: sharon@sharonsiamon.com. Join the crowd!)

COMING IN FALL 2004

Mustang Mountain #7: Free Horse (1-55285-608-9)

Meg is just about to leave the Mustang Mountain Ranch
when Ruby Tucker, owner of a neighboring lodge, falls
ill. Together with Thomas, Meg must help run the lodge
and look after Ruby's rambunctious 10-year-old step-son,
Tyler.

Tyler creates all kinds of trouble when he opens a
gate and lets the ranch horses out. As they search for the
horses, Thomas discovers that someone is catching wild
horses and carting them away. Thomas suspects Tyler's
brother Brett and his friends of selling the horses. As a
hailstorm hits and Thomas fails to return to the lodge,
Meg and Tyler set out on a mission to find him and save
the wild horses.

6

MUSTANG MOUNTAIN
Brave Horse

Sharon Siamon

whitecap

Edited by Lori Burwash
Proofread by Elizabeth McLean
Cover photos by Michael E. Burch (mountains) and
    Mark J. Barrett (horse)
Cover design by Roberta Batchelor
Interior design by Margaret Lee / Bamboo & Silk Design Inc.

Printed and bound in Canada.

National Library of Canada Cataloguing in Publication Data

Siamon, Sharon
  Brave horse / Sharon Siamon.

  (Mustang Mountain ; 6)
  For children aged 8–12.
  ISBN 1-55285-528-7

  1. Rocky Mountains—Juvenile fiction. 2. Horses—Juvenile fiction.
  I. Title. II. Series: Siamon, Sharon. Mustang Mountain ; 6.
PS8587.I225B73 2004   jC813'.54   C2004-900372-0

The publisher acknowledges the support of the Canada Council and the
Cultural Services Branch of the Government of British Columbia in making
this publication possible. We acknowledge the financial support of the
Government of Canada through the Book Publishing Industry Development
Program for our publishing activities.

Please note: Some places mentioned in this book are fictitious while others are not.

To Jordan,
who loves western wildflowers

CONTENTS

Acknowledgments

I'd like to thank the following people for their help in the research and writing of *Brave Horse:*

Lori Burwash, for her excellent and insightful edit as usual;

Dr. Wayne Burwash, an equine practitioner near Calgary, for his helpful advice on horses and their injuries.

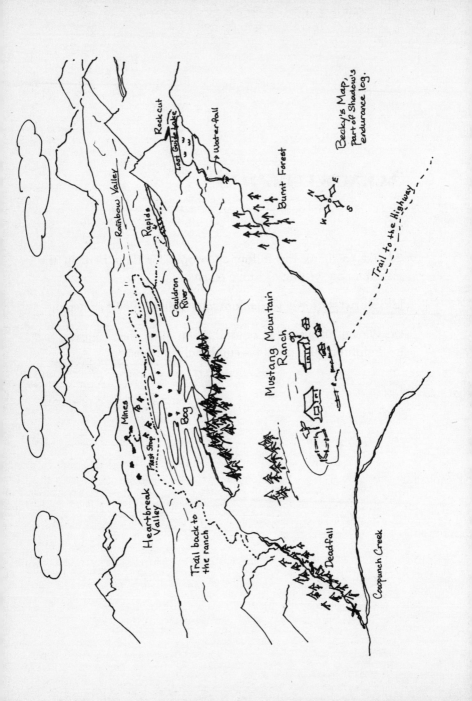

CHAPTER 1

KICK-START

Becky Sandersen bounced on the end of her friend's bed and yanked the covers off her head.

"Wake up, Meg O'Donnell. We've got to be on the trail to Mustang Mountain in less than fifteen minutes."

Meg sat bolt upright. "Wha—What time is it?"

"Six o'clock, sleepyhead. You missed breakfast. But I bought you a peanut butter sandwich to eat in the truck." Becky rattled a paper bag at Meg. "Come on, get up."

Meg's sleepy blue eyes tried to focus. "Stop bouncing! You're making me seasick." Becky's flyaway blonde hair and rosy cheeks looked too wide awake for six o'clock. "Remind me why we're leaving Horner Creek so early?"

"Because I don't want to waste one single second of your visit!" Becky jumped off the bed and spun around

the small motel room. She tore open the curtains, blasting Meg with Alberta sunshine. "Look at it out there. It's perfect trail riding weather. It's perfect weather for having you and Rob and Shadow all to myself at Mustang Mountain Ranch. And best of all," she turned a shining face to Meg, "for once, no cousin Alison to wreck everything."

"I wonder where she is right now." Meg tugged her long brown hair into a ponytail.

"Alison? Probably in some fancy Paris boutique with her dad. Spending money hand over fist, eating snails, flirting with French boys ... who cares? She's not here—that's the important thing."

"It's going to be funny without her." Meg shook her head. For the past two years, the three of them had spent summers at Becky's home, a wilderness ranch high in Alberta's Rocky Mountains.

"Maybe to you." Becky plunked down on Meg's bed. "You didn't have to live with dear lovely Alison—more than a year in New York, with Uncle Roger and Aunt Marion fighting like cats and dogs—then six more months here in Horner Creek after they split up. It's been *torture*. Alison is spoiled, bossy and so conceited she thinks she rules the universe ..." Becky threw up her arms. "Here we go again, talking about *Alison*! Do me a favor, Meg, and don't let her name cross your lips the whole time you're here."

She ran to the bathroom and turned the shower on full blast. "Take your last shower for two weeks. I'm going to go help Mom load Shadow in the trailer."

Becky left Meg humming in a hot shower. There were no showers at Mustang Mountain Ranch because there was no electricity to heat the water. There were also no roads or schools, which is why Becky had been living with her relatives for the school year. But now it was July, and Meg had come from New York for a visit at the ranch.

Becky raced around the corner of the small motel to the parking lot. She found her mother, Laurie, at their banged-up gray truck. She was a small, wiry woman with sun-streaked fair hair and brown eyes like her own.

"Hold up there," Laurie laughed. "You look like you're going to *fly* to Mustang Mountain." She stood back and studied Becky's flushed face. "These months at Horner Creek have done you good," she said. "I've never seen you look so happy."

"It's going home that's making me happy," Becky grinned.

"Could it also have something to do with your boyfriend's comin' to work on the ranch for a while?" Becky's dad, Dan, had been checking the hitch on the horse trailer. Now he straightened up to his full height of six feet and smiled at her.

Becky could feel her face go scarlet. "Rob Kelly is *not* my boyfriend," she shot back at her father. "He's just a good friend."

"Dan, don't tease," Laurie scolded. "You've made her blush."

"I apologize." Dan lifted his hat. "Anyway, Rob's going

13

to be real welcome at Mustang Mountain. We're short-handed this summer—I don't know why it's so hard to get ranch hands to work up there."

"Don't you, Dad?" It was Becky's turn to tease. "Could it be because there are no roads, no cars, no stores or bars, no movies, no TV?"

"Do you think Rob will miss all that stuff?" Laurie asked.

"No, Rob won't care." Becky had met Rob Kelly here in Horner Creek, near Calgary. She knew he dreamed of someday having a wilderness ranch like Mustang Mountain, where the Sandersens raised mountain patrol horses. Rob was going to love it there.

At that moment, Meg came running on her long legs like an awkward colt, her brown ponytail damp and her backpack flopping on her shoulder. "All right, I'm ready to go," she panted.

"That was the world's fastest shower," Becky marveled. "We still haven't loaded Shadow." She ran to the back of the trailer, where a beautiful brown and cream paint mare was munching hay from a hay net. Becky felt a buzz of happiness as she stroked Shadow's silky muzzle. She was really Alison's horse, but Becky had been left in charge of the little mustang for the summer.

"Come on, girl," Becky murmured, untying Shadow's lead rope. "This is your last trip in a trailer for a long time. Then it's mountain trails for you."

Meg helped Becky settle Shadow in the horse trailer. "You know," Meg said, "without Alison we wouldn't

have Shadow and Patch." Alison had adopted the two young mares at a wild horse adoption center in Wyoming last fall.

Becky ran her hand lovingly down Shadow's shoulder. "Shadow is just mine to look after while Alison prances around France. But, yes, it was nice of her to give Patch to you, I have to admit."

Meg had yearned for a horse of her own for years. Now she finally had one. That's why she couldn't stay for the whole summer—she had to go home to work at the stable for Patch's board.

"Let's get this rig on the road!" Becky's dad roared from the front of the truck.

Becky jumped out of the trailer, then carefully closed and locked the door. She and Meg dived into the back seat of the crew cab. Dan and Laurie took the front seat.

Becky kept a close eye on the horse trailer. Shadow hadn't hauled well before—being shut up in the small space spooked her. "The trailer seems to be riding well," she called to her dad. "I hope Shadow's okay."

"Don't worry, darlin'. Another hour or so and we'll be at the trailhead."

Half an hour later, the road left the rolling plains and corkscrewed up a steep hill. Just ahead was the trailhead, with a small corral, an outhouse and an old silver trailer.

Here they would leave the truck and ride the two and a half hours up to the ranch.

Becky looked anxiously for Rob's red pickup. There it was, parked in a stand of pines near the corral. She rolled

down her window and breathed in the warm spicy smell of pine trees, hay and horses. All the misery of the last few months lifted off her shoulders.

Jumping from the truck, she raced back to let Shadow out into the fresh mountain air. But just as she was opening the latch on the trailer door, she heard a sarcastic voice in her ear.

"Hello! I drove up with Rob. Wasn't I *lucky* to catch him?"

Becky whipped around to see a slim girl with a half-embarassed smirk on her proud face. "ALISON!" The weight slammed back down on Becky's shoulders. "What are you doing here?"

CHAPTER 2

PACK STRING

Alison Chant laughed into Becky's furious face. "What's the matter, cuz? Not glad to see me?" Alison had discovered barrel racing while living in Horner Creek and was dressed to fit the role: fitted jeans, a plaid shirt and a leather belt with a big silver buckle.

"What are you doing here?" Becky repeated. The words seemed to blister her lips, she was so angry.

Alison returned her scorching stare. "Rob was coming—I hitched a ride. What's wrong with that? Afraid I'll steal your boyfriend?" She glanced over at Rob, who was helping Dan unload gear from the back of the truck. Like Becky's dad, he was tall and lean, but fair-haired and blue-eyed.

"He's not my boy—," Becky spluttered. "Never mind."

Suddenly her joy in the sunshine and the smell of the pines was gone, swept away by the sight of Alison gazing at Rob as if he were a pair of shoes in a store window. "Just tell me. Why are you here and not in Paris with your dad?"

"It's like I told Rob." Alison batted her long eyelashes in his direction. "I got dumped, like I do every summer." She glanced at her expensive watch. "My parents will be in Vermont by now, at a couples' therapy camp. They've decided to try to work things out. So, where could they send me but here to my Aunt Laurie and Uncle Dan ... and cousin Becky, of course." She reached out her hand to Meg, who'd been standing nearby. "Meg! Tell me you're at least glad to see me."

Meg gulped. She could see how angry Becky was, but poor Alison! She had been abandoned by her parents again, and it must hurt, no matter how she covered up her feelings with that sarcastic smirk. "I'm sorry your trip to Paris with your dad didn't work out," she said.

Alison gave a sad little shrug. "Poor me. I guess it just wasn't meant to be."

Becky wanted to punch her cousin on her small, perfect nose. What a phony! Alison used her parents as an excuse for everything, always playing the poor little rich girl.

"Rob, could you help me get *my horse* out of the trailer?" Alison asked.

Rob straightened up from the pile of gear. "Sure, be right there."

That's the last straw, Becky thought. *Her* horse. She

would have to rub it in. And I hate the way she talks to Rob, as if she has him wrapped around her little finger. She's got a hundred ways to torture me, and she uses them all.

She felt Meg nudge her arm. "C'mon, Hank and Cody are saddled and ready to go. Old Slim brought them down from the ranch last night." Slim was the ranch's cook, an ancient cowboy who'd lived in these mountains all his life.

"There's no hurry now." Becky stomped toward the corral. She knew Meg was trying to smooth over the disaster of Alison's sudden appearance, but it was no use. Everything was spoiled. Behind her, she could already hear Alison arguing with her mother.

Laurie's voice was raised. "Shadow's only four years old, Alison. She's not used to being ridden for two and a half hours. Plus, this trail is new to her. Sorry, we just can't risk it."

"But I've been looking forward to riding Shadow up to the ranch," Alison complained.

"This is one fight Alison's not going to win," Becky muttered. "My mom's the boss when it comes to horses." Laurie was a licensed farrier and an expert horse trainer.

"I really wish you two wouldn't fight," Meg pleaded.

Becky whirled to face her, spots of anger burning in her cheeks. "You didn't have to watch Alison neglecting Shadow at Horner Creek," she shot back. "If Rob and I hadn't rescued her, she might have gone wild again. It was so *typical* of Alison! As soon as we had her trained

and gentled, Alison wanted her back. She said she wanted Shadow for barrel racing, but I know it was really because I was starting to love her." Becky gulped. "On top of that, Shadow's too young for barrel racing!"

"Come on," Meg soothed. "You haven't even said hello to Rob."

"He's busy, helping Alison!" Becky turned her back and strode away.

Meg followed her into the corral. It was made of peeled poles and was just large enough to hold the trail horses that were heading up the mountain. Meg went up beside a tall bay horse called Cody and stroked his rough cheek. Cody brought back such wonderful memories of last summer. "Hello, big fella," she whispered. "I made it back, didn't I?"

Cody lifted his big head and whickered in return. He remembered her! Like all the mountain trail horses, he had strong, sturdy legs. His ended in four white socks and enormous feet. He could travel over the roughest trails, climb over fallen trees and up steep slopes.

And next to him was Hank, Becky's favorite old ranch horse. Meg watched Becky mechanically tighten the girth on Hank's saddle and shorten the stirrups. Her whole body was rigid with resentment.

Meg tried to budge Becky out of her bad mood. "Look at Hank. He has one brown eye and one blue, just like Patch." Her horse, Patch, was a frisky paint mustang, just a little over fourteen hands high, and almost Shadow's twin. How Patch would love it out here, Meg thought,

instead of being stuck in that narrow stall and small pad-dock at Blue Barn Stables in New York.

"If you're trying to cheer me up, it won't work." Becky's cheeks were pale, but there were glints of fire in her brown eyes. "This summer is a wreck already. I won't get to spend any time with Shadow." She gave a wither-ing look over at Alison. "And just look at her, trying to impress Rob."

Having lost to Laurie, Alison was already mounted on Rascal, a dark Appaloosa. She sat tall and straight, her body in perfect balance after years of dressage training. Now she rode Rascal into position behind Rob.

Oh dear, Meg thought, Alison does look beautiful on a horse. "Don't let her get your goat. Ignore her," she mur-mured to Becky.

"I've tried," Becky said miserably. "I tried all winter at Horner Creek. It's useless." She put her foot in the stir-rup and hauled herself onto Hank's back. "You go ahead. I want to ride at the back of the pack string."

"Oh, come on. It's not that bad."

"Yes it is." Becky turned Hank toward the corral gate.

Here we go, Meg thought. I'll be stuck between those two fighting the whole time I'm here. Becky will be like a black storm cloud, shooting lightning bolts, and Alison will just love every second of it. It's what she does when she's bored. I hope something or someone turns up to dis-tract her!

She swung into Cody's saddle and rode out beside Laurie, who was mounted on Mike, a big chestnut with a

white blaze. "Have you heard anything from Thomas?" Meg asked, trying to sound like she didn't care.

"Not a word." Laurie shook her head. "Why? Are you thinking he might turn up at the ranch?"

"He said he would, at the Stampede a few days ago." When Meg first saw Thomas Horne last summer, he had been bending to drink at a mountain stream beside his horse, Palouse, near Mustang Mountain Ranch. When he mounted Palouse and rode off, he'd taken part of Meg's heart with him. All fall and winter, she'd waited for an e-mail from him. Nothing—then, all of a sudden, word that he was going to be at the Calgary Stampede. And when they met again, it was as if no time had passed. She felt this strange connection to Thomas, as though they were tied together with invisible strings. But the strings didn't seem to stretch over long distances.

"If Thomas said he'd come, he probably will." Laurie smiled.

"I don't know," Meg sighed. "Sometimes, I'm not even sure he likes me."

"That's the way it is with these mountain men," laughed Laurie. "I didn't know whether Dan liked me for years, and all the time *he* thought we were engaged. But, hey, you've got lots of time. You're just fifteen, and Thomas is only eighteen."

"That's what he says." Meg remembered a moonlit night last summer when she was fourteen and dying for Thomas to kiss her. But all he did was tell her that she was too young. She remembered his shy smile and dark

eyes, and his shiny black hair, braided down his back in traditional Blackfoot style.

"And this feelin' you have—it isn't one of Alison's in-love-one-minute, out-of-love-the-next kind of things, am I right?"

Meg blushed. "You're right."

"Well, then, if Thomas also feels that strongly, he's probably just tryin' to hold back on gettin' too serious too soon. One thing's for sure. Time will go by, and if it's the real thing, it will last."

"I hope it's real." Meg smiled gratefully at Laurie. It was so easy to talk to Becky's mother.

"Anyway," Laurie went on, "Thomas is welcome. Dan will put him to work—we're so shorthanded right now."

"Becky and I will help," Meg promised. "And I'll bet Alison will, too. She always grumbles, but she works hard."

"I know, but I was hopin' you girls would have time to do some endurance training with my mare, Windy." A shadow passed over Laurie's face. "I need you to do the long distance rides. My back's not up to it."

"I'm sorry!" Meg said. "I didn't know your back was still bad." Laurie had been kicked in the spine while she was shoeing a horse two years ago.

"Well, I'm okay for short rides." She shrugged. "Once Windy's ready for endurance events, I think I'll be able to sit in the saddle all day."

Meg looked up at the snow-capped mountain peaks that loomed in their path. Maybe Laurie didn't consider

this a long ride, but for her, used to a city riding ring, the trail up to Mustang Mountain Ranch was a great adventure. And maybe Thomas would be waiting for her at the other end!

CHAPTER 3

WILD HORSE COUNTRY

The pack string headed up the mountain. They entered a deep pine forest where the trail was narrow and tree branches brushed at their legs. Dan and Laurie rode first, followed by Alison, chattering over her shoulder to Rob. Behind Rob rode Meg, then Slim, with Shadow and two packhorses tied to his saddle.

Becky brought up the rear. As she watched Shadow struggle with the new terrain, her heart went out to the little mustang. The roots and deadfalls in Shadow's path were so different from the open plains of Wyoming where she was born. Shadow snorted, halted and stumbled on the rough trail, starting at every strange noise. Good thing Alison *isn't* riding her! Becky thought. She could hardly see the others through the trees, but she

could hear Alison's high voice ahead in the distance.

"I can't wait to ride Shadow on the mountain meadow. She's going to love it!"

Becky seriously doubted that.

An hour later, they rode out of the forest and down onto a streambed with coarse river rocks underfoot. Dan called a stop to rest the horses before the steepest part of the climb.

Rob led his mount, a buckskin gelding named Sugar, over to where Becky was sitting alone by the stream.

"How are you doin'?" He gave her one of his shy smiles from under his hat brim.

"Do you have to ask?" Becky fired a round stone at the stream. It didn't skip, but sank with a plop. Like my summer, she thought.

"Listen, Becky, I'm kind of disappointed." Rob squatted beside her.

"You mean Alison?" She looked up.

"No, I mean you. I'm sorry to see you go all mopey and miserable again. I thought you two cousins might start to get along."

"You thought wrong." Becky hurled another stone. This one skipped once.

"Too bad." Rob stood and tipped back his hat. "Seems like awfully nice country to be miserable in."

Slim joined them at the stream. Off his horse, he was as bent and gnarled as an old tree stump. He filled a metal cup from where the current ran fastest. "Pretty, isn't it?" he said, waving the cup at the scene in front of

them. "Did Becky tell you that up there is Rainbow Valley, where the wild stallion Wildfire hid his band of mares a couple of summers ago?"

"Really?" Rob glanced down at Becky, sitting like a lump of misery at the water's edge. "Are there still any wild horses left there?"

"Nope, Wildfire was the last of them. Young Thomas Horne saved him from a bounty hunter, then tamed him and took him home. The mares wandered off, I guess. There's still pockets of wildies in these mountains, but none in Rainbow Valley except maybe the ghost of the black devil stallion, Diablo."

Becky pricked up her ears. Was Slim telling this story just to get her out of her bad mood? "I never heard of a ghost horse," she muttered. "Are you sure this isn't one of your tall tales?"

"Well, there haven't been many sightings of that black ghost in the past few years." Slim's weathered face crinkled into a rare smile. "But this spring I've heard rumors that folks have spotted him in Rainbow Valley. Mind you, it's not a place that most people know how to get to."

"But you do." Becky scrambled to her feet, shielded her eyes and looked at the peaks to the west. "You chased Wildfire up there after he kidnapped Windy two years ago, didn't you?"

"Yup," was Slim's short answer.

"What's the story of the ghost horse?" Rob asked. "Why do they call him the devil?"

"Oh, that's just a tall tale, like Becky Sandersen says." Slim started to stroll away. "Looks like I'm needed over there."

Meg and Alison were getting into their saddles. Dan and Laurie were adjusting the loads on the packhorses. They were heading out.

"Are you going to ride with me?" Rob asked. He handed Becky the hat she had tossed to one side.

Becky took a deep breath. She hated Rob to think she was sulking. And out here, in the shadow of the mountains, with the summer sun glinting on the water, her problems with Alison seemed to shrink. "Sure." She smiled at him.

The next hour and a half was a tough climb up a narrow track. Becky kept her eye on Shadow. The little mustang was used to high altitudes in Wyoming, and her hooves were hard and strong. But the trees seemed to spook her, or maybe she was still jittery from the trailer ride. Becky read unhappiness in every line of Shadow's body. It was good she was roped to the packhorses or she might have bolted.

The snow-capped peaks closed in around them, soaring up in cliffs of bare rock. They rode on, climbing steadily, until the country opened into a wider, high mountain bowl.

"Look!" Meg turned in the saddle to shout back to Becky. "There's the burn from the forest fire two years ago." She pointed up to a swath of blackened sticks that had once been trees.

"And there's dear old Mustang Mountain Ranch!" sang out Alison. Below them was the green sloping meadow, the fences and low buildings of the ranch. "Home at last."

It's not *her* home, Becky thought with a sinking heart. The homecoming she'd looked forward to for so long was spoiled.

CHAPTER 4

CAUGHT BETWEEN COUSINS

As they rode into the ranch yard, Meg searched the corrals for Thomas's horse, Palouse, but there was no sign of him. Thomas hadn't come.

She swallowed the sting of disappointment. The ranch looked as lovely and welcoming as ever, Meg thought. The ranch house was a sprawling wood building with a long front porch. Inside was a dining room with a stone fireplace, an office, two bedrooms and a huge kitchen with a cast-iron cook stove.

In the summer, everybody except Dan and Laurie slept in small bunkhouses. Meg, Becky and Alison had theirs, Rob would share his with the other ranch hands and Thomas, if he showed up. Slim had his own little bunkhouse, attached to the woodshed.

They were all hot and dusty after the long ride. After seeing to the horses, they took turns sluicing their faces and hands with cold fresh water from the outdoor pump.

Alison hung around Rob's bunkhouse until he came back from washing.

"I wanted to thank you for driving me up," she said.

Rob scrubbed his wet head with a towel. "No trouble. I was coming anyway."

"That was such a great talk we had on the trail," Alison went on. "You know so much about training horses." They had boarded Shadow at Rob's ranch in Horner Creek. "I'm hoping that you'll have some time to help me train Shadow." She leaned in toward him, reaching for the towel.

Rob straightened up and backed away like a startled horse. "I don't think … I won't have much time … to spend with you," he said bluntly.

Alison was stunned by his refusal. Her eyebrows shot up and her eyes sparkled dangerously. "We'll see about that," she said, walking away.

Before dinner, Rob sought Meg out in the dining room, where she was setting the table. Becky and Alison were helping in the kitchen.

"Hi," he said shyly. "Can we talk?"

Meg had just met Rob at the Calgary Stampede a few days ago and hadn't had a chance to get to know him. These were the first words he'd said to her besides "Hi"

and "Good-bye." She knew that both his parents were dead, and since she had lost her own father many years before, they had at least one thing in common. She also knew that at home he was bossed around by Sara, his older sister. Sara was a barrel racing champion, and it was from her that Alison had caught the racing bug.

Meg saw Rob's Adam's apple slide up and down his skinny throat when he swallowed, and wondered what was coming.

"I don't know how to say this." Rob shuffled from one foot to the other. "It's about Becky, and Alison. I feel like I'm kind of squished between them."

Meg started to laugh.

"What's so funny?"

"I'm sorry. But that's exactly how I feel. I used to say it was like being the filling in a cousin sandwich." Meg chuckled. "No matter what you say, you're going to make somebody mad." She stopped laughing. "Actually, it's not funny. They're jealous of each other, and they make each other miserable."

"Becky doesn't need to be jealous of Alison," Rob said. "She's—I—we're friends," he stammered.

"You mean you like her?" Meg asked. "Becky, that is."

"Sure. We—we ..." Rob was stammering again. "We spent a lot of time together, at my ranch in Horner Creek. You know, training Shadow, and stuff."

"I get the picture." Meg held up her hand. "But what you have to understand is that Alison was always the one who got the guys. Now she's jealous because Becky has

you and she has nobody." She suddenly thought, if Thomas turns up, Alison will really feel like a fifth wheel. She'll just go up in smoke.

Rob saw her anxious look. "Maybe I should leave," he said. "I don't want to make trouble."

Meg grabbed his arm. "Hey! Don't do that. Becky's dad is counting on you to work on the ranch."

Rob nodded. "Maybe Dan'll keep me so busy I'll squeeze out of that sandwich." He grinned at Meg. "Thanks. It's nice to know somebody understands."

Meg sighed. "We all understand Alison. Her parents give her a bad time, and her Grandmother Chant tries to rule her life—but she makes it hard to sympathize."

Becky and Alison had been watching this conversation from the kitchen doorway. Alison was still feeling stung by Rob's rejection. "Those two seem to be hitting it off." She nudged Becky. "See how she grabbed his arm? You'd better watch that Meg doesn't steal your boyfriend."

"Don't be ridiculous." Becky glared at her. "Meg would never try to steal Rob."

"Maybe she wouldn't have to try very hard," Alison teased. "Meg's very attractive since she got so tall. She has those high cheekbones and those blue, blue eyes ..." Alison tipped her head to one side. "They look awfully *natural* together."

Becky's face blazed red. "I'm not going to listen to any more of this. You're nothing but a troublemaker, Alison Chant." She wheeled and stomped back to the kitchen.

Slim was stirring a huge pot of stew on the stove. His nose was red from the heat, and his eyes runny from the smoke. He glanced up at Becky. "What's the matter? You look as mad as Diablo, the ghost stallion."

Becky grabbed a stack of bowls from a shelf. "I don't believe in your silly ghost horse."

Slim shook his head and went back to stirring. "It might be better if it wasn't true," he muttered. "But folks have seen him, this spring."

CHAPTER 5

HORSES AT DAWN

Becky got up very early the next morning. She pulled a sweatshirt over her pajama top, tucked her flyaway blonde hair behind her ears and yanked on jeans and boots. She wanted to get to the barns before Alison could ruin one last piece of homecoming pleasure.

The morning sun was rising over the mountains as she went to look for Breezy. She hadn't seen Night Breeze, as she was properly called, the night before— Breezy had been grazing in the high mountain meadow. It was almost exactly a year ago she was born! Becky thought, remembering that moonlit night.

She found the yearling in a paddock behind the barn. The last time Becky had seen her, Breezy had been a foal running beside her mother, Windy, on long spindly legs.

Could that be her, that sorrel yearling standing by the fence sniffing the wind? Breezy was the first horse Becky had ever loved—even though she'd grown up with horses, an accident when she was very young had made her wary of them. But she had literally yanked Breezy into the world, when Windy was too exhausted to give birth. She'd wiped the foal dry with her sweatshirt and carried her home to the ranch over her saddle through a moonlit wilderness.

She remembered how Breezy would frisk over to her, little bottlebrush tail whizzing around, and bury her slender nose in her pocket, looking for treats. She remembered how sweet the end of that nose smelled. Would Breezy remember?

"Breezy," Becky called out. The filly turned at the sound of Becky's voice and took a few hesitant steps forward.

"It's me," Becky coaxed. "Come and see for yourself."

Suddenly, in the way yearlings have of making a dash, Breezy gobbled up the space between them. At the last second, she planted her forelegs and stopped.

"I've got a treat for you." Becky slid from the fence, inside the corral. "But you have to find it. Remember our game?"

Breezy started sniffing under her arm, in her pants pocket and finally in the top of her boot, where a carrot was hidden. It was as if she'd never stopped playing the game. "Wow!" Becky scratched the top of her head. "You have a sensational memory." She picked up Breezy's

muzzle and kissed the end of her soft nose. "And you still smell good, too."

She climbed back over the fence. "I'm going to go and get Shadow," Becky said. "I want you to meet her." Shadow was the second horse Becky loved. Over the winter, when Alison had ignored the little paint, Becky had taken pity on her and spent hours making friends, then getting her used to the saddle and bridle again. It was hard to remember that Shadow belonged to Alison. Hard to see Alison push Shadow into barrel racing before she was ready.

They had let Shadow out with Windy in a corral on the other side of the long barn. Becky's mother was already there, leaning on the fence, watching the two horses tear at a flake of hay. Becky could remember when she used to resent that look of total love and concentration her mom had when she looked at horses. Now she was beginning to understand. Laurie put an arm around her. "You're up early."

"I've just seen Breezy. She's beautiful!"

"Just like her mother," Laurie laughed. "How would you like to take Windy for a Long Slow Distance ride today?"

"Me? Take Windy?"

"You, and Meg and Alison. Windy needs a lot of LSD as part of her endurance training. I've got a whole program worked out—"

"What do you think of Shadow?" Becky interrupted, knowing that once her mother started talking training schedules for Windy, she could go on for an hour.

Her mother turned her focus to the mustang mare. "I can see why you're so attached to her." She gave Becky's shoulder a squeeze. "She's got an independent spirit."

"You can say that again," Becky sighed. "Remember how she nearly died rather than let herself be captured?" Laurie Sandersen had been in Wyoming when Shadow was adopted.

"I remember," her mother said softly. "She was so skinny and sick—we were all worried she wouldn't make it—but she did! Look at her now. She's small, but beautifully put together. And her color is wonderful."

"Do you think Alison has hurt her, barrel racing her so young?" This was the question that had bothered Becky all spring. She knew what her mother thought of riding a four-year-old hard.

"It wouldn't do her any good." Laurie shook her head. "But Shadow was already a pretty tough little horse, being wild. She'll be okay as long as Alison doesn't push her as hard as she was."

"I think she'd make a wonderful endurance horse, like Windy, don't you?"

Laurie gave her daughter another squeeze. "Maybe. Mustangs have been winning some big endurance races."

"Will you talk to Alison? I think barrel racing's all wrong for Shadow."

"I'll talk to her. But don't break your heart over her, darlin'. You still have Breezy to love and train. And in the end, you have to remember, Shadow is Alison's horse."

"Yes, she's *my* horse." Alison came up behind them.

She was dressed in another new outfit: black jeans, a denim vest and big cowboy hat. "And I'm not interested in any long endurance rides. I want to ride her fast, around barrels. Can we set some up, Aunt Laurie?"

"Not on this ranch, not until Shadow is a year older," Laurie said firmly. "She's just in her fourth year. Why would you want to risk damaging her bones while they're still growing?"

"But she's been out on the range running since she was born!" Alison protested.

"Not with a rider on her back. There's a big difference. She has to learn how to carry you and develop the muscles to do it." Laurie held her ground with her stubborn niece.

"So what am I going to do around here, just sit and vegetate?" Alison glared at Becky and her mother.

"Take one of the ranch horses and go with Becky while she trains Windy. It will be a nice ride."

"A nice, long *slow* ride! A plod, in other words."

Becky bit her lip. She was dying to tell Alison that she didn't need to come, wasn't wanted and could go stuff herself down a gopher hole. But a warning look from her mother made her gulp back the angry words.

CHAPTER 6

LONG SLOW DISTANCE

"I wish I could go with you," Rob said to Becky. He was helping the three girls get ready for their training ride. "Old Slim's been filling me with tales of the things you three have been up to the past two summers. You're lucky to be alive!" Rob grinned. "And, hey, he says to be careful, and watch out for the ghost horse, Diablo!"

"What ghost horse?" Alison hurried over to ask Rob. He repeated Slim's story to Alison and Meg. "He says people have spotted a black horse up in Rainbow Valley," he finished.

"That's fascinating." Alison batted her eyelashes at Rob.

"Oh, you can't believe those old stories." Becky gave Alison an angry glance. "There's no black ghost horse in

Rainbow Valley. Anyway, we're not riding up that way. Mom says to ride downstream and keep to the flats."

They set out at ten. Low clouds clung to the shoulders of the mountain peaks, like streamers of damp fog. Becky led the way on Windy, Meg came next on Cody and Alison rode last, on Rascal, the Appaloosa mare.

"Keep to the flats," Alison muttered under her breath. "Boring, boring, boring." She struggled to keep Rascal in line behind the others. The feisty mare didn't like it, wanted to be in front. "I couldn't agree more," Alison told the mare. "I hate being at the back."

After an hour, they stopped for a rest beside Cowpunch Creek. "Why are we resting?" Alison stormed. "We haven't done anything to get tired!"

Becky sighed. "We have to stop for Windy. In a real endurance race, this would be a vet check," she explained. "A veterinarian would check Windy's condition, her heart rate and body temperature, and make sure she was fit to continue. It's also time to change order," she told Alison. "A good endurance horse doesn't make a fuss about being behind other horses, the way Rascal does."

"What's the order now?" Meg asked. "Cody's happy anywhere."

"You take the lead, Alison," Becky said. "Just don't set too fast a pace."

"Too fast? A two-year-old could ride a tricycle faster. How much longer do we have to do this *Long Slow Distance* stuff?" Alison grumbled.

"Oh, you know what endurance races are like, Alison—twenty-four hours, one hundred miles, one horse, one rider." Becky shrugged.

"You've *got* to be kidding!" Alison looked horrified.

"Yup, I'm kidding." Becky's brown eyes glinted mischievously. "A hundred-mile race is Mom's goal for Windy, but it will take at least two years to get her to that level. Today we're just supposed to ride down to where this creek meets Muskrat River."

They remounted and rode on, following the winding loops of Cowpunch Creek. There were lots of signs of other animals along the trail—elk, moose and grizzly bear. The grizzly signs were the most disturbing—tree stumps torn to shreds by hungry bears searching for grubs, large boulders tossed aside like pebbles along the trail.

At last, in the early afternoon, they reached the junction of Cowpunch Creek and Muskrat River, where they stopped for lunch. The low clouds swirled around them like a soggy blanket. The trees looked black through the mist, and even the river water seemed dark and menacing, running swiftly over smooth river rocks.

Meg, Becky and Alison unpacked their saddlebags and ate in silence—cheese and crackers, fruit cocktail from small cans. The horses grazed on mountain meadow grass.

Meg strolled over to give the horses slices of an extra apple she'd brought.

"Don't give any to Windy," Becky called. "She's not supposed to have anything except grass and her high-energy ration."

"An apple isn't high energy enough for your precious Windy?" snorted Alison.

"Laugh if you like. Mom's training Windy like an athlete. Everything's measured and controlled." Becky was writing down details in Windy's training log.

"But you even write down when she pees!" Alison giggled, looking over her shoulder. "And what color it is!"

"It could be important." Becky slammed the notebook shut. "Are you ready to go back along the creek?"

"Back the way we came?" Alison slumped against Rascal's saddlebag, causing the mare to snort and shy. "That's right, Rascal," Alison said. "You hate the idea of retracing all those plodding steps as much as I do." She hoisted herself into Rascal's saddle and wheeled around. "I'm not doing it. I know where the ranch is, there are still hours and hours of daylight—I'm going back another way."

"Alison, we've been seeing bear signs. Grizzlies. You don't want to tangle with a grizzly bear like you did the summer before last!" Becky glared at her.

"I'll keep my eyes open ..." Alison swung Rascal's head toward the upper slopes. "It's better than dying of boredom."

"Keep away from the trees and rock ledges," Meg called. "Remember the cougar that killed poor old Pie?"

"I'll stay in the open, don't worry." Alison stopped and looked back at them. "Aren't you going to warn me about blizzards, or wildfires? Bogs? Flash floods? Bad guys with guns?"

Becky and Meg glanced at each other. They had faced all those things on Mustang Mountain at one time or another.

"It's the wilderness, you idiot!" Becky shouted at Alison's back as she rode away.

"Should we go after her?" Meg said.

Becky shook her head. "No! It would wreck Mom's training schedule. Besides, it wouldn't do any good. Alison's going to do whatever she wants. Anyhow," she teased, "don't you think we should get back to Mustang Mountain? What if Thomas shows up?"

Meg looked after Alison, who was disappearing into the fog. "Okay, but you just *know* she's going to get into trouble."

Becky swung into Windy's saddle. "Alison thinks she can push the wilderness around, the way she bosses us." She shrugged. "She should know by now that it doesn't work that way!"

But as they headed toward the ranch, Becky felt a stab of guilt. What if something *did* happen to Alison? They shouldn't have let her go off alone.

CHAPTER 7

MEETING IN THE MIST

Alison felt a triumphant burst of energy. She was free of those slowpokes! Heading up a grassy meadow, Rascal stretched out into a lope. They rounded the corner of a hill and looked down on a long, narrow valley to the west.

"Rainbow Valley," Alison gasped. "That's the wild horse valley."

She pulled Rascal to a halt and they stood on the hilltop, the wind ruffling Rascal's mane and Alison's short dark curls. "Should we go and take a look?" She bent forward and stroked Rascal's neck. "Just a short one, then we'll head back to the ranch, okay?"

She let Rascal pick her own way down the rock-strewn slope to the bottom of the valley. There was a stream here, too, and the sides of the valley were high

and steep. They seemed to close in on Alison as she rode Rascal along the streambed. The clop clop of her hooves on the rocks echoed back from the valley walls.

Tree trunks crisscrossed the valley floor in a tangle of deadfall as high as Rascal's knees. "How on earth did Wildfire and the other horses get through this mess?" Alison asked out loud. "It looks impossible."

She began to wonder if entering the valley had been a good idea. It was cougar country, and she was all on her own. It was spooky in here, and the echoes made her ears ring. She hated to give up once she started something, but who would know if she did? She wheeled Rascal's head around and started back the way they'd come.

But there was a horse hazy in the mist at the end of the valley. The rider didn't wave, didn't call out, just sat as motionless and straight as though it was part of the horse.

Too proud to shout, Alison sucked in her breath and kept riding. She'd find out soon enough who it was.

Coming closer, she could see that the horse was an Appaloosa. There was only one other Appaloosa besides Rascal that she knew of up here. "Thomas?" she called out at last. "Is that you?"

"Alison?" Thomas urged Palouse forward. "I thought you might be Meg."

"Sorry to disappoint you!" Alison halted Rascal and sat watching the handsome young man ride toward her. He was at home in these mountains and rode with the ease of his First Nations ancestors. His long black hair

was braided down his back and a lock of his hair was braided into Palouse's mane. Thomas looked as if he'd ridden out of the past, where cities and freeways and high-speed Internet didn't exist.

"Weren't you supposed to be in Paris? What are you doing out here all by yourself?" She could hear the disapproval in his voice. "Where's Meg, and the others?" He looked around, as if Meg might magically appear from behind a rock.

"Paris didn't work out." Alison tossed her head. "And Meg and Becky are poking along Cowpunch Creek at the speed of snails ..." She glared at him. "And you're out here *all by yourself*, I notice."

"That's different." Thomas drew himself up tall and proud on Palouse's back. "I know these mountains. You shouldn't take a horse up that valley. She could get her leg snagged in the deadfall and break it."

"I know that! Why do you think I'm coming back?" Alison was furious with him, acting as if she was completely clueless. She suddenly had an idea of how to wipe that smug expression off his face. "I wanted to take a look at Rainbow Valley," she said. "Isn't this where Wildfire hid his band of mares?"

Thomas nodded.

"I heard there's another wild horse in Rainbow Valley."

"Another wild horse?"

She had his full attention now.

"Who told you that?" Thomas slipped from Palouse's back and let the gelding drink from the stream. He was

trying to act casual, but Alison could see the excitement in his face.

"Old Slim, the cook at Mustang Mountain." Alison hopped off Rascal. "I don't think Slim's seen him himself, but he claims other people have. He said he's a fabulous black stallion that runs like the wind."

Thomas stared at her. "Another wild stallion? I've never heard of him. Are you sure?"

"Yes, but this one is much wilder and stronger than Wildfire, Slim says." Alison looked sideways at Thomas. Would he really believe this story?

"Maybe I should take a look." Thomas's dark eyes were shining with excitement. He was swallowing all of it! Alison knew he had a dream of protecting the wild horses that were left in the mountains. He was starting a herd of his own, sired by Wildfire. A bigger, stronger horse was irresistible.

"Do you want me to come with you?" she asked. "After all, it might not be safe to be all alone up there … and what about the deadfall? Your horse might get snagged, you know."

Thomas didn't like to be teased. He just shook his head and gathered Palouse's reins. "We'll get through the deadfall, don't worry." He leaped into the saddle. "I was on my way to Mustang Mountain," he said. "Tell Meg I'll get there in a couple of days. I'll just check out this horse first."

Alison gulped. A couple of *days*! What had she done? Meg would die if she knew Thomas came this close and

went chasing off after a horse for two days. An imaginary horse! "Do you have enough food and stuff for a ride like that?" she asked. "Maybe you should come to the ranch first."

"We're okay." Thomas patted Palouse's saddlebag. "I always carry extra supplies." He glanced at Alison. His eyes were steady and serious. "Listen, if a friend of mine, Charles McClintock, comes along, tell him I'll catch up with him later."

"You have a friend c-coming to Mustang Mountain?" Alison stammered. "Should we tell him to wait for you? Stop—" She clutched at Thomas's leg.

"Don't worry about it." Thomas reached down and loosened her grip. "Charles and I will meet up somewhere else."

He urged Palouse around with a gentle cluck and rode up the narrow valley without another word.

Alison stared after him. If Thomas's friend was anything like Thomas, he'd be something special. Meg could have Thomas, Becky could have Rob. She would have this new, wonderful man. *Charles*. He'd probably be tall, and quiet, like Thomas. Maybe he'd have hair that fell across his forehead like a raven's wing.

But she had ruined everything. She'd sent Thomas on a wild goose chase after a ghost horse.

CHAPTER 8

COWPUNCH CREEK

Alison held up her hand and started to shout. But the cry died in her throat. How could she call Thomas back and confess that she'd sent him off to chase a phantom horse? He'd be so disgusted with her.

Her big mouth was always getting her in trouble. If only Thomas hadn't been so smug, so superior! Alison flung herself on Rascal's back and set off back toward Cowpunch Creek in a fierce mood.

Why did things turn out this way every time! she wondered. Why did Meg and Becky have boyfriends, but not her? Especially Meg! When they'd first become friends two years ago, Meg was plain and dumpy and thrilled to be asked to join Alison's elite riding school. She, Alison Chant, had taken Meg under her wing and

fulfilled all her dreams, even inviting her for the summer to Mustang Mountain.

But Meg had totally betrayed her by growing tall and gorgeous. She had not only learned to ride, she turned out to have this *gift* with horses that everybody was so thrilled about. Big deal! So she could communicate with horses. Worse, much worse, was her effect on guys. Last summer, every guy they met, including Thomas Horne, hadn't been able to take his eyes off Meg. Some friend she'd turned out to be!

Alison urged Rascal into a jog along the narrow trail by Cowpunch Creek. They could all go to blazes!

A low cloud lay close to the creek, making it hard to see very far ahead. But twenty minutes later, she glimpsed Meg and Becky, still plodding slowly along the stream. She pulled Rascal up short. Had they heard her coming? No, they didn't seem to be turning around—they were riding side by side, deep in conversation.

Alison felt a pang of jealousy. Probably sharing boyfriend experiences! She slid off Rascal's back and led her to the stream to drink. What'll I tell them? Alison wondered. I can never admit I saw Thomas and sent him off looking for an imaginary horse. But they're bound to find out sooner or later. She sank beside the creek with her head in her hands.

A rustle in the brush behind made her suddenly stiffen.

A bear? Off her horse and sitting down, she was in a horribly vulnerable position. She opened her mouth to scream for Becky and Meg.

*

"I *do* feel sorry for her," Becky was saying as they walked their horses along the creek. "My Aunt Marion and Uncle Roger are always too tied up in their own troubles to have time for Alison. And then there's that rich old dragon, Grandmother Chant, trying to bribe Alison into being as snobby and stuck up as she is!" Living in Alison's house in New York, Becky had seen Alison's grandmother in action.

"Do you think they'll stay together?" Meg asked. "Alison's parents, I mean."

"I don't know. I'm not sure it's even a good thing if they do. They never do anything but fight. But it will be good for Alison when it's all decided and done with. She must feel like a yo-yo, pulled between New York and Horner Creek."

"What will you do about school if Alison ends up in New York?"

"I don't know. Maybe stay on the ranch and take correspondence courses." Becky made a sour face. "One thing's for sure—I'm not going back to school in the east." She glanced at Meg. "Sorry, Meggie, but I've had enough of your snob school in New York!" At Alison and Meg's private school, Becky had felt as out of place as a cactus in a rose garden!

"I wouldn't want to go back either if my mom wasn't there, and my brother David ... and Patch," sighed Meg. "There are so many things I love about the west—the mountains and the clear air and ..."

"And Thomas?" Becky teased.

Meg didn't smile. She tugged at her ponytail and shook her head. "I think that's why he hasn't come," she said in a low voice.

"What do you mean?" Becky looked sharply at her friend. "What's the matter? Did you and Thomas have a fight at the Stampede?"

"Not exactly a fight." Meg's glance was unhappy. "But ... I think I was too pushy ... I was so glad to see him." She brushed a strand of hair out of her eyes. "It's probably best. When Thomas is around, I can't see straight, or think straight, or even hear what people are saying to me. I think I imagined stuff that wasn't true."

Becky nodded. She remembered Meg and Thomas at the Calgary Stampede. When she was near Thomas, Meg wasn't aware of the crowds, the midway, the music or the rodeo going on in front of them. "Did he kiss you?" she asked.

"No," Meg sighed. "No, he didn't."

Alison clamped her hand over her mouth to keep from giggling as a droopy brown nose poked out of the bushes behind her. It wasn't a bear—it was a moose. Just a calf by the looks of him. All legs and a goofy expression.

But in the next second, Alison scrambled to her feet. A huge cow moose, ears laid back and murder in her eyes, was bearing down on her at a fast trot from the other side of the creek.

Alison had heard Becky's father say that a moose's sharp front feet could slash a horse to ribbons in a few seconds.

"C'mon, Rascal!" Alison grabbed for her reins. "We've got to get out of here."

But Rascal wasn't waiting. Mountain horses hated the very smell of moose. She gave one terrified neigh and raced away, leaving Alison behind.

In mud or muskeg, Rascal might have been in trouble. But on dry ground, she could outrun a moose, even though they run amazingly fast. The moose gave up and turned. Alison was still between her and her calf. She lowered her head and charged.

Alison screamed. There was no way to scramble out of range of those flashing hooves. She took off her hat, waved it and shouted, at the same time trying to clamber up the side of the creek valley, away from the calf.

It was no use. The moose kept coming. There was fury in her small dark eyes. Alison crouched, shielding her head with her hat, trying to curl up in a ball.

What happened next was so sudden and astonishing Alison could never be sure what she'd seen. Hoofbeats pounded down the streambed. A huge black animal came thundering out of the fog, dashed between Alison and the onrushing moose, hurling a challenge over its shoulder.

Confused, the moose shuddered to a stop, shook her head and charged off after this new danger, her calf bawling after her.

Alison lay limp as a rag, waiting for her breathing to

return to normal. She was lucky to be alive! Was that a black horse? Where had it come from?

Lucky or not, Alison realized she was now in real trouble. Rascal was gone, it would take her hours to walk all the way back to the ranch, and there were still bears and cougars in the area, let alone moose!

"HELP!" she bellowed, hoping Meg and Becky were within earshot.

CHAPTER 9

RETURN TO THE RANCH

Becky turned at the sound of Alison's shout for help.
"Did you hear something?"

A minute later, Rascal came galloping toward them,
her reins dangling, her mouth frothing, clearly terrified.

"What's happened?" Becky threw herself off Windy
and made a grab for Rascal's reins. "Rascal, you dumb
horse. What have you done with Alison?"

"I knew she'd get in trouble," Meg cried.

"You were right," said Becky. "We'll have to go back
for her, but I don't want to ride Windy that fast." She
mounted Rascal in one fluid motion. "Take Windy's lead
rope and tie it to your saddle."

Meg nodded and watched Becky and Rascal disappear around a bend in the creek. "Here, Windy," Meg

said, tying the little mare behind Cody. "We could probably let you free to walk beside us, but you never know what we're going to find up there."

Windy whinnied as if she understood. She was such an intelligent mare, Meg thought. You could talk to her and almost swear she understood. The only time Meg had ever seen her hard to control was when Wildfire had stolen her from the ranch two summers before. Then, she'd been a different horse, determined to run with the wild stallion.

Leading Windy, Meg rode down the streambed until she heard voices around the next bend. It was Alison, coming toward her on Rascal, with Becky striding beside her.

"What happened?" Meg gasped. Alison was pale and rumpled, her face and hair smudged with dirt.

"I was attacked ..." Alison began.

"She has a story you just won't believe," Becky burst out.

"Go ahead, don't believe me." Alison was shaking. "That horse, or whatever it was, saved my life."

"From a moose," Becky said, starting to giggle.

"Laugh if you like." Alison pulled herself up straight in the saddle. "I hope you get charged by a two-ton moose someday. See how you like it."

"You said a horse," Meg urged. "What about the horse?"

"It was huge, and black. It galloped down the creek just as that moose was about to stomp me into the mud and chased her off."

They were both staring at Alison in total disbelief.

Becky finally untied Windy's rope from Meg's saddle. She stroked the mare's nose. "We can take our time getting back," she said. "The whole schedule's shot now."

"I'm sorry," Alison mumbled.

"Well, you don't have to go making up stories about ghost horses and a monster moose just to make yourself feel better about racing off and wrecking Mom's training schedule. Slim's story about Diablo has got you hallucinating." Becky climbed into Windy's saddle without looking at her cousin.

"I didn't say it was a ghost horse," protested Alison. "I don't know what it was. I couldn't see."

She glanced at Meg, but Meg's blue eyes were clouded with doubt. That's it! Alison thought, quivering with fury. I'm not going to mention meeting Thomas. Maybe he'll stay in Rainbow Valley and never even show up at the ranch. Why get into any more trouble than I have to? And maybe he'll discover that the black horse was not a ghost or a phantom. Whatever saved me from the mother moose was real enough!

It was a long, silent ride back to Mustang Mountain Ranch. When they got there, Alison unsaddled Rascal and stalked off to visit Shadow without another word. While Meg went to the ranch house to see if there was word about Thomas, Becky sat on a bale of straw, recording Windy's training ride in the log.

Meg came rushing back into the shadowy barn. "There's bad news," she gasped.

"Thomas—?" Becky lifted her eyes from the log.

"No, it's Rob. He got bucked off a green horse and smacked his head on a fence post. He's in his bunkhouse now."

Becky threw the notebook and pencil aside and dashed from the barn with Meg at her side. Alison saw them running and hurried from the corral. They crowded into the bunkhouse, where Rob lay pale and flat on his narrow bunk, watched over by Laurie.

"My first day on the job," Rob groaned as Becky bent over him. "I was tryin' to show your dad I knew my way around horses. One minute I was sitting on that horse, and the next I was in midair!"

"*Horses!*" Becky put a lot of passion into the word. "I love Breezy and Shadow, and there's a few like Hank I trust, but the rest of them are miserable, untrustworthy— Mom, is he going to be all right?"

"He'll be fine," Becky's mother promised her. "But he should stay still, and we'll watch for signs of concussion."

"I'll watch," Becky said. All her fear for Rob came rushing back. He'd been recovering from mono when she first met him, but she didn't know that, and for months she'd imagined he had something horribly wrong with him. He still looked too frail to be a ranch hand.

Rob's eyelids were drooping. "You rest," Becky said. "But I'll be here to make sure you don't sleep too long." She motioned for Meg and Alison to leave.

Later, it was a sad group that gathered around the long ranch table.

"Are you sure Rob will be okay?" Becky asked her mom. "He seems awfully sleepy."

"You mean, should we send for a helicopter?" Laurie shook her head. "I don't think so." Rescue helicopters were Mustang Mountain's connection to the outside world of doctors and hospitals—to be used only for emergencies, like when Laurie was kicked. "Rob hasn't broken anything that I can tell. But he'll need to rest for a couple of days."

"I'm sorry the boy got hurt," Dan sighed. "On top of that, I'm a hand short again, and there's so much work to do."

"I wish Thomas would come," Meg said shyly. "He would help."

Alison thought about Thomas out in Rainbow Valley and the horse she'd seen. If Meg knew I sent Thomas off after an imaginary horse, she'd slaughter me! Alison told herself.

She got up and wandered outside to the veranda. The sky had cleared and stars winked above the snow-capped peaks.

Slim was sitting on a bench, smoking a pipe. He looked up and motioned for Alison to sit beside him.

"I hear you saw Diablo today." He puffed on his pipe.

"I saw something that looked like a dark horse," Alison said. "It was huge and black as night." It was a relief that somebody believed her, even if it was a crazy old cowboy. She sighed. "Whatever it was, it saved my life, I know that."

"I'm not surprised," Slim said, "being that you're a girl."

"What does that mean?" Alison plunked down on the bench beside him.

"Well, just that if you'd been a boy, he might have stomped you like a rattlesnake. Diablo hates men. They chased him up here from the Mexican border, those old mustangers, but none of them could get a rope on him. At last they gave up and rode off south. Diablo stayed. He was the bravest horse I ever heard of. For years, every wild horse hunter around here tried to catch him. Some of the meaner ones tried to crease his neck with a rifle bullet to slow him down."

"That's cruel!" Alison shuddered. "Shooting a horse just to catch it. Did they really do that?"

"Some of the mustangers were cruel men." Slim nodded. "They shot at Diablo, but they couldn't slow him down. Finally, a big gang of men trapped him at the end of the valley, and there was nowhere for Diablo to go but into their lassos or over the cliff."

"So he jumped?" Alison found herself imagining the big black horse, weary from all the running, poised on the cliff top.

"Yup. He'd rather die than let those men catch him. That's courage." Slim banged out his pipe on the veranda and the live sparks flickered in the air. "But a lot of people say his ghost lives on. They say his ghost'll try to kill a man if it can. That's how he got his name, Diablo—the devil horse."

"But why does he like girls?" Alison was curious. She didn't believe in ghosts, but this was an interesting story.

Just then the screen door banged open.

It was Becky, with Meg behind her. "I'm going to check on Rob again," Becky told Alison. "I want to make sure he's not sleeping too much."

Meg banged the screen door shut. "I'll go with you."

The two of them slipped off the veranda and ran in the direction of Rob's bunkhouse, where a single light bulb lit the door.

"I get the idea our Becky is kinda sweet on that youngster." Slim pointed his pipe at the bunkhouse. "Oh well, I guess it's her age. You got a young fella, too?"

"No." Alison felt a yawning loneliness sweep over her. "There's no one I care about." It is so true, she thought miserably. I don't really love my crazy parents, and who could love my Grandmother Chant? Becky hates me, and now Meg, my closest friend, has abandoned me.

Alison brushed her misery aside. "You were going to tell me why Diablo likes girls." Even listening to an old horse story was better than thinking about her life.

CHAPTER 10

RED-HEADED STRANGER

"It's too long a story for this time of night." Old Slim yawned. "I've been up since before dawn. Ask me again some other time." He got stiffly to his feet, banged out his pipe again and headed inside for a last mug of coffee.

Alison headed for the barn, where Shadow was stabled. Most of the horses were out, but Laurie had decided to keep Shadow inside at night until she settled down from her trip up the mountain and got used to her new surroundings. As she opened the barn door, Alison caught the sweet, familiar smell of hay and horses. She switched on the dim overhead light and walked down the center aisle to Shadow's stall.

"How're you doing, little girl?" Alison whispered, stepping into the stall and reaching up to stroke Shadow's

forehead. "Are you lonely, too?" Shadow whinnied and poked Alison in the shoulder with her hard nose. "You must miss Patch." The two horses had been inseparable before their capture last fall. "I know everything feels strange here, and I'll bet you wonder whose horse you are, Becky's or mine."

Did horses think about who they belonged to? Alison asked herself. Probably not! "Well, anyway, you're *my* horse, and I'm going to spend more time with you, I promise," Alison told her. "If they won't let me ride you, I'll bring you along when we go out riding so you don't get stale and bored." It was so unfair of Laurie not to let her ride Shadow on the trails. She'd been *barrel racing* Shadow this spring, and that was a lot harder than trail riding! Laurie was a tyrant about horse training.

She gave Shadow a final pat, turned off the light and headed for her bunkhouse without waiting for Meg and Becky. When they came in, chattering about Rob, she pulled the covers over her head and pretended to be asleep.

"I wish I knew what happened to Thomas," she heard Meg sigh as she switched off the light by her bunk.

Alison felt a stab of worry. Could it be true what Slim said? That there was a ghost horse who hated men? Would kill them if it could? Surely it was all just a dumb old story, and yet *something* had chased off the moose. Alison clenched her sheet around her chin. It was too late now to confess she'd sent Thomas into Rainbow Valley. She hoped he'd turn up tomorrow.

*

But it was not Thomas who turned up in the morning.

Chores were finished and Alison was slinging plates on the table for breakfast when someone thumped on the door.

"Howdy!" The door banged open. A voice boomed through the ranch house, "I'm looking for Thomas Horne. Would he be here?"

Meg and Becky rushed to the kitchen door at the mention of Thomas's name.

Alison stared. This must be Thomas's friend. But he didn't fit the image she'd conjured up at all. He wasn't quiet, or raven-haired, or anything like Thomas. When he took off his hat, she saw that he had bright red hair and lots of it. He was tall, but he was also chunky through his neck and shoulders and waist. His shirt was as red as his hair, and his jeans baggy.

He clumped across the ranch house floor in a heavy stride and reached for Alison's hand. "I'm Chuck McClintock." Closer up, Alison saw that he had freckles totally covering his face and a wide, irritating grin.

"Thomas isn't here." Alison tried to sound aloof.

Chuck grabbed her hand in his big paw and pumped her arm up and down. "That's funny," he said in a voice that would carry to the barn. "He said he'd meet me at Mustang Mountain Ranch, yesterday or today."

Meg came forward. "Thomas is coming? You're supposed to meet him?"

"That was the plan." Chuck grinned. "Hey, didn't he

tell you about me—his best buddy, Chuck McClintock?"

"I thought Thomas said your name was Charles." Alison's hand flew up to her mouth. She knew at once what she had done. Meg stared at her.

"Chuck, Charles, same name," Chuck was saying. "So which one of you girls is Meg?"

Meg glanced quickly at him. "Me. I'm Meg." She turned to Alison again. "When did Thomas talk to you about Chuck?"

Alison had a horrible, trapped feeling. They were all staring at her.

"Alison?" Meg's eyes were steely blue. "*How come you knew about Chuck*?"

"Because I saw Thomas yesterday," Alison blurted defiantly. "At the entrance to Rainbow Valley."

Her words fell like bricks. In the silence, she could hear the neighing of a horse in the yard.

"Why didn't you say something?" Meg gasped.

"You wouldn't believe me about the moose. Why would you believe me about Thomas?"

"Oh, come on. That's completely different," Becky burst out angrily. "You didn't tell her out of just plain spite." Her voice rose. "Alison Chant, how could you?"

"I almost get trampled by a moose and you don't blink an eye." Alison stood with her hands on her hips. "Thomas goes riding off after a horse and everybody acts like the world's come to an end."

"What horse?" Becky, Meg and Chuck asked in unison.

CHAPTER 11

ALISON WORRIES

"The black horse that saved me from the moose, the one I told you about." Alison knew she was playing with the truth. Thomas had gone off searching for the black horse *before* she saw it, or even believed it existed. It seemed a harmless enough lie, and it had a wonderful effect.

"So, there *was* a real horse." Meg's shoulders relaxed. "Of course, he would want to go and look for it."

Even Chuck looked satisfied with her story. "Rainbow Valley, eh?" He scrubbed his shaggy head with thick fingers. "Yeah, Thomas told me about that place. Well, if he's gone hunting for horses, he won't be back for a day or two."

"Will you stick around and wait for him?" Meg asked eagerly. "I'm sure the Sandersens won't mind."

Say no! Alison pleaded silently. She wanted no part of this big oaf.

"I guess I might, especially if there's work I could do around here."

Becky beamed. "There's work, all right. My dad's shorthanded right now."

Chuck sucked in a big breath and threw back his broad shoulders. "Sure. I'll stay. If you want me to." He winked at Alison.

Oh no! Alison groaned to herself. Not a winker!

"I'll go set another place for breakfast." Meg paused and put a hand on Alison's shoulder. "I wish you'd told me about Thomas, but I guess I understand," she said with a shake of her brown ponytail. "I'm sorry we laughed at you."

"That's all right." Meg's forgiveness made Alison feel guiltier than ever.

Everybody but Alison seemed pleased to have Chuck stay. She didn't like the way he talked, or laughed, or took over the conversation. After breakfast, he said, "I suppose none of you girls would like to wash a load of laundry for me? I've been on the road for a while, and my socks and underwear are getting kind of rank."

Alison glared at him. "Sorry! You can wash your own smelly socks."

"I'll do it for you," Becky volunteered. "I know how to make our cranky old washer work off that generator."

"Thanks." Chuck grinned. "Thomas said you were a nice girl."

"Where do you live?" Meg rested her chin on her hand and gazed at Chuck's freckled face. "And how do you know Thomas?"

"I'm from down around Kananaskis, west of Calgary," Chuck told her. "I worked with Thomas on a ranch there one summer."

"You guys are so young and you've done so much," Meg marveled.

"Ranch kids out here, like Thomas and Rob and me, start working around the place when we're nine or ten," Becky pointed out. "We're old hands by seventeen or eighteen."

Chuck beamed at her. "You got that right."

The next two days were busy at Mustang Mountain Ranch. There were chores, Windy's endurance training and working with Shadow and Breezy. Rob was let out of bed on the second day and appeared in the corral, pale, but steady on his feet. Becky hovered around him like a mother hen.

Meg watched anxiously for Thomas to appear.

As for Alison, she tried to stay out of Chuck's way. He seemed to have the annoying idea that they should be friends and kept shoving his big freckled face into hers and asking dumb questions.

"Where'd you learn to ride like that?" he shouted at her across the corral when she was riding Shadow in slow figure eights.

"In the circus," Alison shot back. She wasn't going to tell him that she'd almost been a junior dressage champion. He probably wouldn't even know what dressage was!

"Why are you avoiding me?" Chuck followed her into the barn after her ride. "There must be something about me you like?"

Alison rolled her eyes at him. There was nothing about Chuck that was even faintly appealing, from his battered boots to the chunks of red hair that stuck out under his hat. "The only thing I like about you is your horse." She nodded at his sorrel gelding, Copper, visible through the open barn door. "He's a beauty."

"Copper is my pride and joy," Chuck agreed. "He has some mustang in him, like your little paint mare. They make great trail horses, don't they? Hey! Why are you making that face?"

"Because Shadow is a barrel racing horse, not a trail horse. Only I can't race her here—Laurie thinks she's too young!"

"She should know." Chuck shrugged. "Thomas spoke highly of Mrs. S. He said she was one of the best horse people he'd ever met."

"Oh." Alison raised an eyebrow at him. "What did Thomas say about me?"

"Not much." Chuck grinned his maddening grin. "Just that you were fairly good-looking. And used to getting your own way. He said he was sorry you weren't going to be here because he thought you and I would get along so well." Chuck winked. "But, hey! Here you are

after all. What happened to your trip to Paris, anyway?"

"None of your business!" Alison flung at him. This was so humiliating. Did everybody have to know she'd been dumped by her dad? "I can't imagine why Thomas would think we'd get along," she told him with her nose in the air. "You're not my type. By the way, why did he call you Charles?"

"It's a joke," Chuck laughed. "I started calling him Tommy, just to bug him. So he calls me Charles. You have to admit, I'm not the *Charles* type."

"No," Alison gave an exaggerated sigh, "sadly, you are not."

"Well, I guess I'll just have to find a way to impress you in spite of my name." Chuck was still grinning.

Alison turned her back on him and led Shadow away. "Don't waste your time. It's not going to happen."

But Chuck's conversation got her thinking about Thomas. He *had* meant to come to Mustang Mountain Ranch and see Meg. So what had happened to him? Was he still chasing a wild horse? She wished she'd never had that sudden wicked impulse to send him up Rainbow Valley. Why, why, why hadn't she kept her mouth shut?

Finally, she tackled Slim again on the porch after dinner.

"Thomas said there was another route into Rainbow Valley." She swung one leg over the porch railing and perched on it. "Do you know it?"

Slim puffed on his pipe. "Suppose I did?"

"The route you showed us is all clogged with dead-

fall. If we wanted to go looking for Thomas, we'd need another way into the valley."

"And why would you go looking for Thomas? Seems to me, that young fella can look after himself."

"But he's chasing that black horse I saw ..."

"Diablo's ghost?" Slim squinted up at her. "You never told me that!"

"I'm not sure it *was* a ghost horse." Alison paused. "And Thomas wouldn't think so."

"He could be in a lot of trouble, chasing Diablo." Slim shook his head. "How long has he been gone?"

"Three days."

Slim stood and shook the stiffness out of his legs. "That's long enough. If you want to go look for him, I'll come along and show you the way."

CHAPTER 12

THOMAS TRAVELS

Thomas woke at first light. This was the third night he'd slept out on the trail. He rolled over and felt the sharp stones under his blanket. The air was heavy with morning dew and the smell of pine. He could hear his horse munching grass nearby.

He whistled but Palouse didn't come. Then Thomas remembered that he had hobbled him—tied his legs so he couldn't run away. Normally, he'd just leave him free to graze, knowing he would stay close, even protect him if danger threatened. But something had spooked Palouse in Rainbow Valley. At night he was restless and nervous.

Thomas got up and untied the big Appaloosa. "What's the matter, my friend?" he whispered in his horse's ear. "Is it a cougar you're worried about, or wolves? Or is it that

wild horse we've been chasing?" He smoothed Palouse's mane and stroked his side. "Come on, let's get a drink."

The wild horse was out there—Thomas could feel it. He didn't want to catch him, at least not on this trip. But he was determined to see the horse up close and make contact. "I'm a good tracker," Thomas was still speaking to Palouse, "but I just can't get near enough to that black horse to get a close look at him."

Clouds hung heavy over the river near Thomas's camp. He and his horse bent to drink where the current was swift. Up here in the high valley, the water was cool and clear and flowed fast over the rocks. The best-tasting water in the world, Thomas thought, straight from a glacier. He took a long drink from his cupped hands and let the rest of the icy water run through his fingers. As he lifted his head, a shape, swirling in the mist on the other side of the river, caught his eye. There was no sound, no clatter of hooves on stone, no snort or whinny, but definitely the shape of a horse.

Thomas slowly rose to his feet. He could be soundless, too. He ran back to roll up his blanket and grab his saddle and bridle. The shape had disappeared by the time he swung into the saddle, but he splashed across the river on Palouse's back and headed into the mist.

"One more day," he told his horse. "My food's getting low, and I promised Meg I'd get to Mustang Mountain, but I hate to give up now. We'll follow him one more day."

∗

All night, Alison dreamed of the black horse as a whirling dark force that threatened to crush everything in its path. When Thomas didn't show up the next morning, she tackled Becky and Meg in the barn, while they groomed the horses. "Slim says three days is *much* too long for Thomas to be gone." She exaggerated to make her idea sound more forceful. "He says he'll go with us to look for him."

"Why are you getting Meg all worried?" Becky tried to get Breezy to stand still in the cross ties and submit to a good brushing. Meg was grooming Windy, and Alison was working on Shadow's gleaming hide.

"Because if I get Meg worried, you'll do something. If it's just me, nobody will pay attention. They never do."

"Poor little Alison," Becky mocked.

Alison felt the bitter sting in Becky's words. Her cousin often lost her temper, but she wasn't usually so sarcastic. What was eating her? Alison thought she knew—she'd taken Shadow away when Becky was counting on having her for the summer. "I think we should go look for Thomas. I'll ride Shadow," she threw back at Becky.

"You know what Mom said about riding Shadow!" Becky glared at her over Breezy's back.

"Stop that, you two," Meg interrupted. "*Should* I be worried about Thomas?"

"This is the fourth day he's been up in that valley, alone. Something could have happened to him." Alison shook her dark curls. She didn't want to tell them why

she was really worried, didn't want to mention that the black horse could be a man-killer.

"We promised Mom we'd take Windy on an LSD ride today." Becky put down her brush and looked thoughtfully at Meg.

"Could we go in the direction of Rainbow Valley?" Meg asked.

"Slim says there's an easier way into the valley ..." Alison put in. This was looking hopeful.

"Thomas can look after himself in the wilderness." Becky glared at her. "Unlike *some* people I could mention! Look, I've got the training route all mapped out for today, but if Thomas still doesn't turn up, I'll talk to Mom. Maybe we could all go tomorrow—Chuck and Rob, too."

"Not Chuck!" Alison exploded, giving an angry swipe of the brush at Shadow's neck.

Becky winced. Shadow was sensitive to people's feelings—Alison's angry words would upset her. And it was *mean* of her to treat Chuck the way she did. "Why not?" she asked, smoothing Shadow's mane. "He's Thomas's friend, and for some strange reason he seems to like you."

"She's right," Meg agreed. "Chuck always tries to sit with you, and his eyes follow you wherever you go." She grinned. "I think he's nice."

"Nice?" Alison spluttered. "He's a big clumsy oaf. I wish he'd just leave me alone!" She tossed her grooming tools in a bucket and started toward the tack room.

Meg and Becky looked at each other and sighed.

"She's right about one thing," Meg said. "Somebody should be looking for Thomas. It is too long."

"Tomorrow," Becky promised. "Don't worry, Meggie. He knows what he's doing out there. Any time now, he'll come riding into the ranch on Palouse with a great story to tell."

Alison was still within earshot and felt a shiver dance up her spine at Becky's words. What story *would* Thomas tell when he appeared? I don't care if it gets me in trouble, she thought rebelliously. Just as long as he's all right.

Thomas followed the black shadow through the clouds of mist that clung to the mountains. He had never known such a creature. Usually, if a horse was alone, it would get tired of being chased after three days and be curious about who was behind him. This horse just kept moving, tirelessly, as if it had a destination. Up and down hills and across rivers Thomas followed him on Palouse. But sometimes, he would find they had traveled in a huge circle. It was as though the black stallion was playing a game with him.

He rode out of the clouds at mid-morning and found himself on the edge of a bog of gray muskeg that stretched across the valley floor. Under the tufts of grass and shrub lay black ooze that could suck a horse to its death. It was not a place Thomas had been before.

"Hold up," he spoke softly to Palouse. "No way we're crossing this."

But ahead of him, he saw the black shape of the horse, running lightly across the bog as if he knew exactly where it was solid enough to hold him. How could he do that? Was the ground firmer than it looked?

"Too dangerous." Thomas shook his head. "We'll go around."

The muskeg spread like the arms of a giant octopus into every low-lying crease of the land. Pine and spruce, too thick to ride through, grew down close to the bog. It took hours for Thomas to thread his way around the edge, pressing Palouse close to the trees and being careful not to let him take one step into the sucking mud.

By the time they reached the spot where the black horse crossed the muskeg, it was already late afternoon. Here, the ground rose to a ridge, and the trees grew farther apart. Thomas urged his tired horse upward.

There was another valley beyond the ridge, even more remote than Rainbow Valley. It was surrounded by bare mountain slopes, pockmarked and pitted with dark holes, like caves.

"Old mine tunnels," Thomas breathed, surprised he'd come so far. "This must be Heartbreak Valley." From this distance, the tunnels looked like groundhog holes, with a fan-shaped heap of dirt below each one. Many years ago, there had been a small gold rush in the area. Prospectors had rushed in to search for gold, silver and other precious minerals. All of them had gone broke and left their mine workings like open wounds on the mountainsides.

It was a bleak, lonely place, and dangerous, Thomas

knew. The piles of loose crushed rock from the mines could suddenly come sliding down on a horse and rider. There were hidden pits and shafts everywhere.

"I don't believe the black horse came this way," Thomas told Palouse. There seemed to be no other way out of the bowl-shaped valley, and no creek or spring in the bottom.

"No water." Thomas shook his head. "Nothing can live here."

He was about to turn Palouse's head for the long trek back down the ridge and around the muskeg when a flicker of movement on the other side of the valley caught his eye.

It was the black stallion, as plain as day, prancing along a high ledge toward one of the mines that tunneled into the rock.

"We can't come this far without one last try, Palouse," Thomas cried, urging his horse down the slope at a jog into Heartbreak Valley.

CHAPTER 13

TRAPPED

It was as if the black horse was waiting for him. Thomas would catch glimpses of him as he crossed the valley and rode up the ledge. But from this angle, the ledge was in dark shadow, and if the horse was there, he blended into the black rock.

Only the fact that Palouse was sure-footed made the climb possible. Loose stones skittered out from under his hooves and clattered down the gravel slope. "This must have been an old tramway to the mine," Thomas muttered to himself, seeing signs where the solid rock had been chipped away to make a path for small ore cars.

Now it was no wider than an animal trail, and in places the outside edge had been worn away by rain and snow, making it even narrower. Palouse had to press

against the rock wall and step carefully to avoid sliding down the steep incline.

"We shouldn't have come up here," Thomas gasped, seeing that, not too far ahead, the ledge seemed to vanish. He must have been wrong—the black horse was nowhere in sight. If it had climbed the ledge, it would be standing right there, where the tramway narrowed to a point at a jutting rampart of rock. Thomas began to worry about how he would get Palouse turned around and back down.

To his relief, the tramway ended at a tunnel dynamited by the miners. No telling how deep it went back into the mountain. The opening itself was shored up with old timbers forming a roof and walls on either side. The timber frame was leaning, bent by the enormous weight of rock around it.

"But it should hold up long enough for us to get turned around," Thomas told Palouse. "I don't know about you, my friend, but I'll be glad to see the last of this place."

A raven croaked his hoarse call as Thomas rode into the tunnel's mouth. Palouse's hooves rang on the rock floor. He gave a startled snort in the sudden darkness of the tunnel.

"Steady, boy. We're all right."

Thomas could hear water dripping nearby. The timbers holding up the tunnel were wet and smelled of rot. He took a firm grip on Palouse's reins. "Time to get out of here."

But at that moment there was a pounding of hooves on the ledge outside. A great black horse reared up in the tunnel opening, pawing at the mine frame. Palouse

whinnied in fear and reared to meet the threat. Between the two horses, the rotting timbers came thundering down, and with them large chunks of loose rock.

Thomas threw up his arms to shield his head. Dust filled the chamber, choking and blinding him. He clung to Palouse's neck and waited for the cave-in to finish them off.

*

After dinner, Dan Sandersen spread a map on the long kitchen table. It showed every hill, stream, swamp and trail in the area.

Meg pointed to symbols on the map. "What are those crossed hammers?"

"Those are old mine workings," Dan said. "Abandoned for years. But it's unlikely Thomas would be away up there in Heartbreak Valley. The way I remember the place, there's no water or grazing for horses."

He drew his finger across the map to Rainbow Valley. "Here's the narrow end that you pass on the way up to the ranch," he told them. "That's where all the deadfall is."

"Slim knows an easier way into the valley," said Alison. Chuck leaned over her shoulder to see and she shoved him away. "Back off!" she growled. "Quit leaning over me."

"Just trying to look at the map." Chuck grinned.

"Well, look at it from the other side of the table. I don't like you breathing in my ear."

Alison pointed to a round blue splotch on the map.

"Here's Lost Guide Lake. Remember when Wildfire was guiding us away from the fire two summers ago?" Becky and Meg nodded. The memory was scorched into their brains. Beautiful little Lost Guide Lake had been their salvation!

"And remember how, when the helicopter landed, Wildfire took off with the mares and disappeared at the end of the valley?"

Laurie gave a rueful nod. "One of those mares was my Windy."

"Well, Slim says there's a trail into Rainbow Valley from there," Alison went on. "When they went to get Windy back, that's how they got in and out. We could get into Rainbow Valley the same way, without climbing over all that deadfall."

Becky glanced at her mother. "Is that too tough a trail for Windy now that we're training her for endurance?"

"I don't think so. Take enough supplies for two days," her mother advised. "And watch her. If she's getting sweaty and breathing hard, stop. Take an extra horse. And at the first sign of lameness, change horses."

"We'll take Shadow," Alison said. "She'll love a trip like this."

"Mom already said we can't ride Shadow on the trails," Becky stormed. "And who says she'd love it? She was spooked all the way up the mountain."

"And how is she ever going to get used to the terrain if we never take her out in it?" Alison shot back.

"Mom?" Becky appealed.

Laurie looked from one angry girl to the other. "Alison's got a point," she admitted. "You can take Shadow as the extra horse." She was tired of arguing with her stubborn niece about Shadow. "Just keep your eye on her."

Alison threw Becky a look of triumph. "I can take care of my horse."

"I gather Slim's going with you, as a guide," murmured Dan.

"He said he would." Meg nodded, glad the argument about Shadow was over for the moment.

"I'll go along, too," Chuck offered. "Thomas is my friend, and if he's in trouble it'll take more than three girls and an old guy to get him out."

Mister know-it-all! Alison opened her mouth to argue.

Becky cut her off. "That's a great idea!" She looked up at her father. "What about Rob? Can he come, too?" Rob was off mending fences. He'd been working hard to make up for the time he'd spent recuperating.

Dan sighed. "It wouldn't hurt him to get the lay of the land either. Just come back here as quick as you can."

"Thanks, Dad." Becky threw her arms around his neck. "Mom, help us plan the ride. We'll start first thing in the morning."

CHAPTER 14

READY TO RIDE

"Are you sure your dad's all right with me going?" Rob was coiling a length of rope in the barn, getting ready to tie it to the saddle.

Becky nodded her golden head. "He says it's a good way for you to get to know the country. Hold still, Molly!" She was trying to tie a pack on the brown mare's back, but Molly was dancing around, making it difficult.

Becky tightened a final knot and stepped back to admire her work. Molly's pack was balanced well, tied with crisscrossed ropes in the way her dad had taught her.

"You're a lot more relaxed around horses than you used to be." Rob smiled at her.

"Thanks to you." Becky felt her cheeks starting to glow. "You helped me work with Shadow when she and I

were both scared and jumpy." Somewhere, deep inside, the old wariness of horses was still there, Becky knew, but a good mountain horse like Molly was nothing to be scared of.

And Rob's praise meant a lot to her. He had never told her directly that he liked her—they talked about horses instead. But there's hope, Becky thought. Alison's attempt to cause trouble between them hadn't changed the special smile he seemed to smile only at her. Especially when they were alone like this.

To stop the blush from taking over her whole face, she changed the subject. "What do you think of Chuck?" she asked.

Rob's smile faded. "There's something funny about him."

"Alison hates him. She says he's loud and pushy."

"I think that's all an act," Rob said. "What bothers me is that when I asked him about where in Kananaskis he lived, he clammed right up. Wouldn't talk about it. I'll bet he doesn't even come from there."

"But why would he lie about such a simple thing?" Becky frowned.

Rob shrugged. "That's what I mean. There's something not quite right. And he never talks about himself—notice that?"

Becky smiled. "You don't either." But she tucked it away in her mind, this feeling about Chuck. Could Rob be right?

✱

"I can't believe you're really Thomas's friend," Alison was telling Chuck in another part of the barn, where she was getting Rascal and Shadow ready. "You are *nothing* like him."

"What do you mean?" Chuck wore his most annoying grin. When he smiled like that, his cheeks puffed out in two perfectly round freckled balls.

"Thomas is quiet and dignified and, and ..." She searched for the perfect word to describe Thomas. "Graceful, in a way."

"I can be graceful. Watch this!" Chuck did a fake ballet step, throwing out his arms and making Shadow snort and shy.

"Stop that! I'm trying to get her calmed down." Alison shoved Chuck aside. "Oh, I really wish you weren't coming!"

"You'll change your mind when you see what a good tracker I am," said Chuck. "Thomas taught me everything he knows." He picked up his saddle and settled it on Copper's back.

"I doubt that. Anyway, Slim is our tracker."

"I thought Slim was a cook!" Chuck reached under Copper's belly for the cinch.

"He's a cook now. But he was a cowboy for years, and he knows these mountains better than anyone. Certainly better than you."

"Why don't you like me, Miss High and Mighty?" Chuck asked, tightening the cinch.

"Let me give you a list," Alison shot back. "One,

you're conceited, although I can't imagine why! Two, you haven't stopped bothering me since you got here. And three, you are not my type."

"Three good reasons." Chuck came close to her, his face serious. "All right, I'll stop bothering you, I promise. If you tell me what you *really* saw out there that sent Thomas off up Rainbow Valley."

"I can't!" Alison ducked under Rascal's neck to groom her other side. "Sometimes I'm sure it was just a black horse. Sometimes I don't know what to think. It might have been a black horse. It might not ... it appeared and disappeared so suddenly." She shivered.

"Well, if you can't tell me, then I can't stop bothering you." Chuck beamed at Alison over Rascal's withers. "There's something you're hiding. I can see it in your face whenever Thomas is mentioned."

Alison turned her back on him. She hadn't told the others that if Slim was right, the ghost horse was a man-killer. She was worried, but she hadn't realized it showed in her face.

She strode off to where Rob and Becky were working. Their ease with each other made her suddenly furious. "I'm really glad you're coming, Rob," she flirted. "We'll have lots of time to talk on the trail, like we did on the ride up to Mustang Mountain." She sauntered away before he could answer, but not before she caught a glimpse of Becky's angry face.

*

Meg was packing for the ride in the bunkhouse. It was important to take everything they needed, *but nothing extra*. Just one blanket for sleeping and a Mylar sheet to keep out the rain and wind. This could be tightly rolled inside rain gear and tied on the back of her saddle. Extra plastic bags to pack out garbage—nothing should be left on the trail except their footprints. Water bottle, energy bars and, this made Meg gulp, a first aid box, in case Thomas was hurt.

She checked her mental wilderness survival list: a hatchet for cutting firewood, waterproof matches, fishing line and hooks, a folding knife ...

Laurie tapped on the screen door and let herself in.

"All set?" she asked.

Meg nodded. "Almost."

"Try not to worry too much." Laurie wrapped Meg in a warm hug. "Thomas is pretty strong and wise for his age. And he's done a lot of wilderness trekking."

"I know," Meg sighed. Becky's mom always seemed to understand what she was feeling. "But his only weak spot is wild horses. He wants to save them all. I worry he might do something crazy if there was a horse involved." She remembered the year before, when Thomas had ridden with a gunshot wound in his arm to bring Wildfire safely back to the ranch.

"That's right. And *your* only weak spot is Thomas Horne." Laurie smiled. "So don't go running off and doing something crazy to rescue him. Promise me you'll use your very excellent good sense out there."

"I promise." Meg smiled back as Laurie gave her a final hug and left the bunkhouse. But Meg knew in her heart that if Thomas was in trouble she would do anything, *anything* to save him. Their time together was quickly running out. Before she knew it, she'd be flying home to New York and the small suburban town where Patch was waiting at Blue Barn. It all seemed unreal, that other world.

Meg zipped up her pack and headed for the door. What was real was here, the mountains, and Thomas, somewhere out there. She needed to find him, to know he was safe and still cared about her!

CHAPTER 15

Burnt Forest

Thomas lay unconscious in the mine tunnel. The dust had settled. Pieces of the broken timber lay at crazy angles in the small space.

Palouse stood over Thomas, as if to protect him, his head lowered, his eyes shut. He seemed to understand it was important not to stamp or whinny. Any jar could bring down tons of rock on their heads.

Light filtered in through gaps in the fallen rocks at the tunnel mouth. It was morning. Palouse nudged Thomas gently with his nose, but Thomas made no sound, so Palouse went back to standing still, waiting for him to wake up.

*

At Mustang Mountain Ranch, Laurie had last-minute tips for the riders setting out. "Don't wait until you're thirsty to drink. By that time, you're already dehydrated and not thinking clearly. Same goes for the horses. Give them plenty of water."

Becky pointed to the water bottles hung around her waist pack and attached to the saddle. "Don't worry, we had the water lecture in Wyoming, didn't we, Alison?"

Alison made a face at her. "Drink, drink, drink, I know." She'd had altitude sickness in Wyoming and it was a nightmare!

"When you're resting, take off their bridles and let them munch all the grass they want. There's plenty of water in it. And if there's a stream, let them stand in the running water—it's good for their legs. Unless they're very tired or night is coming—then they might get a chill," said Laurie. "I guess that's about it."

Becky patted her saddlebag. "I packed first aid supplies for the horses."

"Good. And you've got Slim with you, so I know you'll eat well," Laurie sighed. "Well, you'd better get going. Good luck."

The six of them rode out of the ranch yard. Becky on Windy first, followed by Meg on Cody and Alison on Rascal, with Shadow tied behind. Chuck and Rob rode side by side, Rob on Sugar, the buckskin, Chuck on Copper, gleaming like a new penny. Old Slim was in back on his big mule, Agnes, leading the pack horse, Molly. The morning was cool, and clouds threatened over the mountains.

The first part of their ride was a slow upward climb. When they reached the pine forest, where trees grew close together, Alison felt a sudden tug on the rope holding Shadow. She turned to see the mare with her feet planted and her ears back. "They're just trees," Alison soothed. "Come on, girl." She kept up a stream of encouraging talk to Shadow as they wound up the mountain, and it seemed to help.

Soon they came to the burnt-out area of the forest fire. Dead trees stood like blackened fingers. The three girls were silent, each one remembering the roar of the flames, the choking smoke, the fierce heat of the fire two summers before.

As they rode through this barren, black world, Chuck thought he saw something moving out of the corner of his eye. "Look," he called to Alison, "did you see that?"

"What?" Alison peered through the stand of tightly packed black tree trunks.

"For a second I thought I saw a horse, running in and out of the trees—a black horse."

Alison looked hard, but whatever Chuck had seen had vanished. From behind her, Shadow gave a whinny. When she looked back, Shadow had her ears flattened once more, and Alison could see the whites of her eyes, as if she was terrified of something.

Alison felt a shiver run through her. Was the ghost horse along on this trip? She shook the thought away with an angry toss of her head. "I don't really believe in ghosts," she told herself. "Ghost horses or any other

kind." But the feeling of something moving along beside them, watching them, wouldn't go away.

Here and there, patches of small trees and wildflowers brightened the dark landscape. In the end, the forest would be renewed by the fire—young trees would have lots of sunlight; the ashes would provide minerals for growth.

But for now, the ground was still covered in charred trunks and blackened rocks.

There was a stream flowing down through the burn, but no one suggested stopping to rest the horses. None of them were sorry when they reached the end of the burn. Ahead, the stream trickled down a steep bluff in a thin waterfall. At the top of the rocky bluff was Lost Guide Lake.

"We should get off and walk the horses up this," Becky announced. "It's too steep to ride."

Old Slim shook his head. "I think Agnes and I can make it if we take it slow," he said, and the two of them took off up the rocky slope, with Slim still in the saddle.

Chuck laughed. "I guess there's no rules for those two stubborn old mules."

Becky slid from her saddle. "This is a good place to practice tailing with Windy."

"What's tailing?" Meg asked.

"She tows me up the steep part with her tail," Becky explained. "In endurance races, that's sometimes easier on the horse than carrying a rider. Watch, I'll show you."

She pulled a thin cotton line from her pack and

attached it to one side of Windy's bit, then ran it back through the stirrup. She grabbed Windy's long, thick tail in her other hand and urged the mare forward. "Come on, girl," she cried. "I hope this works," she threw over her shoulder to Meg. "It's one thing to practice this in the corral, and another to do it on a slope this steep!"

Soon Windy was scrambling up the bluff, pulling Becky behind her.

"Doesn't that hurt her tail?" Meg asked doubtfully. She was climbing the rocky slope beside Cody, letting him choose his own path.

"Nope. A horse can pull a lot of weight from its tail ..." Becky let go as they reached the top. "I guess it could be useful in a long race." She sat down in a heap. "To tell you the truth, Meggie, I wish I was riding Hank. It's a lot of responsibility having Windy on this trip. Mom will kill me if anything happens to her."

"Nothing's going to happen." Meg wiped her sweaty brow. "We're going to find Thomas, that's all ..."

As Meg's voice trailed off, Becky realized her friend was choked with emotion. "You're scared, aren't you? About Thomas."

Meg bit her lip and shrugged. "I just have this bad feeling. I can't explain it, but everything seems so confused. We're all supposed to be trying to find him, but Alison's fighting with Chuck and you're worried about Windy."

Becky stood up. "I'm sorry." She put a comforting arm around Meg's shoulder. "You're right. We should focus on

finding Thomas." She looked down the slope, where Alison, Chuck and Rob were still struggling. "If you ask me, this all has to do with Alison."

"Oh, come on," Meg protested.

"No, let me finish," said Becky. "Alison's like a vortex sucking everything down. It was going to be such a wonderful time till she came." Becky glanced at Meg with troubled eyes. "You have to admit, she spoiled our first training ride, and maybe we would have met Thomas if she hadn't tangled with the moose and told him about the black horse and … oh, I don't know! Somehow it all seems like her fault."

"Becky," Meg said gently, "you always think things are Alison's fault."

"But sometimes they are!" Becky cried. "Look at her right now, screaming at the top of her lungs at poor Chuck. I know she's worried about her parents and hates the world, but somehow she manages to spread her trouble around and get us all mixed up in it!"

Meg was about to say something, but Alison's shout interrupted. "You kicked that rock right into my leg!" she roared at Chuck. "Why can't you watch what you're doing?!"

Chuck paid no attention to Alison. "Holy catfish!" he exclaimed. "Would you look at that!"

CHAPTER 16

LOST GUIDE LAKE

It was Chuck's first sight of Lost Guide Lake. He took off his hat, rubbed his head and gaped in wonder.

Becky, Meg and Old Slim, who had seen the lake before, grinned at Chuck and Rob, standing speechless with amazement at the scene in front of them. Small and beautiful, Lost Guide Lake was almost perfectly round. The water was a deep turquoise, reflecting the soaring walls of rock that surrounded it.

"It's just an old glacial lake, for heaven's sake," Alison was muttering as she finally scrambled up the last few steps leading Rascal and Shadow. "Somebody could have helped me with Shadow—I practically had to *drag* her!" Shadow had balked and fussed the whole way up. Now she stood tossing her mane in the wind,

scanning the meadow that sloped down to the lake. She'd never seen a big body of water like this. All her senses were on high alert.

"You're the one who wanted to bring Shadow," Becky muttered. "So don't complain about it."

"She needs the exercise." Alison raised an eyebrow at her cousin. "*Somebody* has to look after her, you know."

Becky ground her teeth. All the times Alison had neglected Shadow last fall and winter, and now she had the nerve to say that! Meg shot her a warning look. All right. No more arguments. Focus on finding Thomas. Becky straightened her shoulders.

"We should give the horses a rest and have something to eat and drink ourselves. It's still a long way to Rainbow Valley."

"Sounds good to me," Slim said. "Break out the rations."

They rode their horses down to the lakeshore, then took off their saddles and bridles to let them drink, graze and roll. Shadow had to be coaxed to go near the water, startled by her reflection in the crystal clear water. Finally, she dipped her nose and drank with the others.

Meanwhile, the riders ate mouthfuls of trail mix, drank energy drinks and gazed at the lake, held like a jewel in a ring of mountains. Slim lay back on the grass, his hat over his eyes to snooze. Even Alison stopped sniping at Chuck, awed by the immense silence of the wilderness.

"No wonder you remember this place." Rob's blue eyes glowed with delight. This was the wilderness he'd been looking forward to—this hidden valley with its

blue-green lake. "Which way do we go from here?"

Meg pointed down the bowl-shaped valley. "We ride to the end, and there's a narrow passage under a rock overhang," she explained. She didn't add that on their last trip through the passage a cougar had leaped on a horse named Pie and slaughtered it before any of them could save him. "According to the map," she went on, "once we're through the rock cut, we ride down into the Cauldron River valley and then Rainbow Valley will be over the next ridge."

Becky stood up and dug in the saddlebag for her training log. "While we're eating, I'm going to do a simulated vet check on Windy." She flipped open the book. "Besides the tests I did last time, the vet would check her for lameness when she trots and for signs of dehydration or stress." She glanced at Meg. "Don't worry, it won't take long."

She ran through a few tests, pinching Windy's skin to make sure it didn't "tent up," running her hands down her legs to make sure they weren't hot, checking for rubbed spots under the saddle. Even a small rub at this stage could get serious on a long ride. But Windy's hide glistened with good health. So far, she seemed in excellent condition.

"Endurance races are always in miles," Becky told Meg, making calculations in her book. "I figure if we ride to Rainbow Valley tonight, that will be about thirteen miles. And the trip back tomorrow will make it about twenty-six in two days. That's as long as a short race."

"What about if we have to go farther—to find Thomas?" Meg asked in a small voice.

"We'll see." Becky frowned. "I hope it doesn't come to that."

Stomachs full, horses saddled and ready to go once more, the six of them set out for the rock cut at the other end of the lake.

This was easy going. Alison handed Shadow's lead rope to Meg. "Let's have a gallop down the meadow," she shouted as she, Rob and Chuck urged their horses into a hard run along the lakeshore.

Becky held Windy back. "Running flat out's not in the training program for this ride. She can do short gallops, but not on a long ride like this."

"I'll stay with you," agreed Meg.

"What are those three young fools doing?" Old Slim watched them getting farther and farther ahead. "It's not good to split up like this."

"Maybe they'll wait for us at the rock cut," Becky sighed. "You can't gallop through that." She was stung by Rob racing off and leaving her, but he was so excited to be riding in this wilderness paradise that she forgave him. It *was* beautiful!

But at the passage, there was no sign of the three of them. Becky, Meg and Slim squeezed their horses into the narrow cut, formed thousands of years ago by glacial water carving through the rock. There was just room for the horses to go single file.

Shadow stamped her feet and whinnied, unhappy

about being closed in. Terrible memories of the squeeze chute at the adoption center in Wyoming made her fearful of narrow places with high sides.

"Alison and the others must be way ahead of us," Meg groaned, as they struggled with Shadow. "I wish they hadn't ridden off and left us."

"Alison again," Becky muttered. "Just what she wants, getting the two guys off by herself. Troublemaker!"

CHAPTER 17

SWEPT AWAY

Once through the long rock cut, Alison, Rob and Chuck pulled up their horses and looked at the Cauldron River that boiled through the narrow valley below.

Later in the year, this would be a shallow stream, running clear over gravel beds. Now, although it was past the spring floods, water was still high.

"See anywhere good to cross?" Chuck asked.

"Maybe we should wait for Becky and the others." Rob looked over his shoulder. He hadn't meant to get so far ahead, but Sugar had enjoyed the gallop.

"Oh, Becky will be doing her pokey old endurance thing," grumbled Alison. "She could be ages. Let's at least wait down by the river, so the horses can drink." She was excited that Rob had agreed to ride ahead with

her. Maybe he was starting to thaw. Now, if they could just lose Chuck!

A stand of young jack pines grew along the river. As they rode into it, Chuck, who was in the lead, shouted, "There's that horse again!" He urged Copper forward and they headed off through the trees.

Alison glanced at Rob. "Did you see a horse?"

Rob shook his head.

"Neither did I. I think we should go after him." Alison was suddenly frightened. She'd wished Chuck gone, but not to chase a ghost!

Ahead, Chuck bent low over Copper's neck as branches whipped his face, making it hard to see. Close to the water, the trees grew even thicker. He caught flashes of a black horse dodging swiftly in and out of the pines, changing direction, blending with the dark trunks.

"You must be the tricky devil Thomas is chasing," Chuck panted. "Maybe you'll lead me to him—in any case, I'm going to catch you. Let's get him, Copper!"

Copper was a skilled cow horse, used to dodging after cattle. This was a challenge he enjoyed.

And then, suddenly, they were at the river. Chuck caught a glimpse of a dark head swimming in the swift-flowing water.

"Come on, Copper, old boy!" Chuck shouted, and they plunged into the river.

Copper scrabbled at the gravel bottom, trying to get his footing. The current was fast, the water deeper as he neared the middle of the river.

In the next moment, they were bowled over by a rush of water. Copper lost his footing and they were swept away downstream.

Chuck fought to keep his head above water, free his feet from the stirrups. If he stayed on Copper's back, he could drown. Ahead, the waves were higher and the water rushed and foamed around black, shiny boulders.

Chuck felt Copper slam into one of these boulders. He went under as his horse slid away from him. Now he was on his own, fighting for air as the river tumbled him over and over like a scrap of driftwood. His boots and heavy clothing weighted him down like a stone.

Again he went under and fought his way to the surface, weaker this time. Ahead he glimpsed a tree trunk slanting into the river. It might be his last chance—if he could just catch hold of it!

CHAPTER 18

WHERE IS COPPER?

Alison and Rob heard Chuck's cries above the roar of the river.

"He jumped in without looking for a safe place to cross!" Rob's face was pale. "What's the matter with him?"

"I know what's the matter with him!" Terror clogged Alison's throat. "He's chasing that blasted horse."

The two of them made a final dash through the thick jack pines to the river's edge. Far downstream they could see something clinging to a fallen tree.

"I think it's Chuck!" Alison pointed. "He's down there. Come on!"

The trees grew in a dense mat along the riverbank. They could go faster if they ran on foot.

Alison jumped off Rascal's back and tied her lead

rope around a tree trunk. Rob was already reaching for the coil of rope on his saddle.

"Hurry!" Alison cried over her shoulder.

"I'm gonna need this." Rob freed the rope and ran after her.

They thrashed through the pine and poplar trees. Alison felt as though she were in a dream where her legs refused to move fast enough. They could no longer hear Chuck shouting.

At last they came to the fallen pine tree. The river boiled under and over it, shaking it like a dog shakes a stick.

"There he is," Alison screamed. "There's his arm."

They could see a white hand gripping a small branch on the tree trunk, and Chuck's head, appearing and then disappearing under the foam.

"Chuck, we're coming, hold on!" she shouted as loudly as she could, cupping her hands so he could hear over the thunder of the river.

Rob tied a loop in one end of the rope. "I'll crawl out there and try to get it around his shoulders," he told Alison. "You take this end and help pull him in. I won't be able to pull much till I get back off the slippery trunk."

Alison nodded, her dark eyes wide. She watched Rob flatten himself on the trunk and inch toward Chuck.

"Hurry, hurry," she whispered. If Chuck let go, they would lose him. Inwardly, Alison apologized for all the put-downs and mean things she'd said to Chuck. They seemed so babyish and unimportant now.

Rob was struggling to get the rope around Chuck, who was too weak to help himself. For one heart-stopping moment, Alison thought Rob was slipping off the trunk into the rapids. "Hold on!" she screamed. She saw him right himself and try again to get the loop over Chuck's head and shoulders with one hand.

Seconds crawled by, with nothing but the sound of the river raging in her ears. Then, "Pull!" she heard Rob yell, and with all her might, she heaved on the rope. Rob was scrambling back up the trunk toward her. He grabbed the rope in front of her and together they yanked Chuck's body free of the greedy current and toward the shore.

A few seconds later, he was on his hands and knees at the river's edge, coughing and spluttering and spitting up water. His red hair was plastered to his head and his freckles stood out on his white cheeks. His eyes were bloodshot with water and strain as he stared up at Alison and Rob.

"Copper," he croaked. "My horse. Did you see him?"

"Sorry ... no." Rob was still panting hard from the effort of dragging Chuck free of the rapids.

"We were trying not to lose sight of you," Alison choked. "We didn't look for Copper. I'm so sorry, Chuck." She meant it. This was a nightmare.

"I've got to go after him." Chuck staggered to his feet. "Can I take your horse, Rob?"

Rob grabbed his arm to steady him. "Shouldn't you wait ... till you catch your breath? You nearly didn't make it, buddy."

"Can't waste time. Where are your horses?" Chuck looked wildly around for the buckskin.

"We left them back there." Alison pointed upriver. "The trees were too thick …"

Chuck didn't wait to hear her explanation. His boots squelching water, he flung himself back along the riverbank to where Alison and Rob had tied their horses. He was already in Sugar's saddle by the time they caught up to him.

"I'm going to ride higher up, out of these trees, where I can make better time," he told them. "Copper will be far downriver by now. I've got to find him."

"I should come with you," Rob said. He glanced at Alison. Both of them knew Chuck was in shock—in no state to go riding off alone. But they had only two horses.

"Take Rascal." Alison moved swiftly. She untied Rascal's lead rope and thrust it into Rob's hands.

"What will you do?" Rob swung up into the saddle and looked down at her pale face.

"I'll go back up on the ridge and wait for Meg and the others. Rob," she begged him, "I know I've acted like an idiot, but I'll be all right."

Chuck was already urging Sugar forward through the thicket of trees. "Please just take Rascal and go!" Alison was frantic. "Hurry! Chuck's likely to do something crazy, like go back into that river to save Copper."

"All right." Rob swung away. "Be careful."

"*You* be careful!" Alison gulped back her fears. She hated to be left alone out here, with no horse. But this

was all her fault! The black horse had appeared from nowhere to rescue her from the charging moose. But whatever had lured Chuck into that river was no friendly force. It must be Old Slim's devil horse, Diablo. She knew now for certain it was real!

CHAPTER 19

SLIM'S STORY

"You see what I told you," Slim muttered to Alison. "It's Diablo all right." He cracked a stick over his knee. "He's got rid of all the boys—first Thomas, now Chuck and that other fella. Just me left now."

Alison had met Becky, Meg and Slim at the top of the ridge. They had waited until dark for Rob and Chuck to return, but there was no sign of the boys or the horses. Then Slim had insisted on making camp, getting a fire going and preparing a meal.

Becky paced by the fire. "Shouldn't we go looking for them?" she urged. "Alison says Chuck was half-drowned when he went riding off."

But Slim just shrugged his skinny shoulders. "It's no use gettin' your knickers in a knot," he said kindly.

"Those are long rough rapids in Cauldron River there," he motioned to the river below, "and it's a long, sad business lookin' for a horse in them." He gazed off into the darkness. "If we have a fire goin', they'll find us a lot easier on their way back."

Meg was thinking about Thomas. This was the fifth night since Alison had seen him. Something was wrong. She felt it like a sickness inside.

They were all quiet with their thoughts, while the fire crackled in front of them and the stars came out over their heads.

"I don't understand," Alison said finally, looking at Slim. "Why did the black horse lead Chuck into the river?" She gave the pot of beans on the fire a stir. "Why would he want to hurt Chuck? He *helped* me when I got charged by a moose."

"Sure, but, like I told you before, you're a girl, like Gretchen."

"Who's Gretchen?" Meg and Alison asked together.

Slim squatted beside the fire, where he could keep an eye on the coffee pot so it wouldn't boil over. "She was a girl, looked something like Alison, here, but younger, maybe eight years old. She came up with her folks to settle around these parts in the eighteen nineties ..."

"That's over a hundred years ago!" Alison exclaimed.

"Not so long if you're seventy-three, like me," Slim said. "Do you want to hear about Gretchen and Diablo, or are you gonna keep breakin' my train of thought every five seconds?"

"I won't. I'm sorry," Alison mumbled.

"All right, then. This child Gretchen was trouble." Old Slim glared at Alison. "Always yakkin' and fightin' with her five sisters and brothers and worrying her folks. They were traveling in a horse-drawn wagon up to their new homestead, and in that wagon was everything they owned, plus the six kids. Little Gretchen was the worst of them, forever fightin' like I said, and pestering her pa to let her ride their old mare.

"She pestered and fussed until one day her pa finally let her sit on the mare's back and follow along behind the wagon. That horse had great big bags of grain tied to each side, so there was nowhere for Gretchen's feet to hang down. It was like a platform up there, and her pa had to tie her on so she wouldn't fall off."

Slim took the lid off the coffee pot and gave it a stir. "They went along fine, until the wagon got a wheel stuck in a gully and the axle broke. They stopped to fix it. By this time, the sun was hot and Gretchen had fallen asleep, still tied on the mare. So she didn't notice when the mare wandered away down a draw to graze, and neither did anyone else.

"After the wagon was repaired, they realized Silky and Gretchen were missing. They followed her trail down the draw and found a maze of mustang tracks in the sand. They made camp to search for her, just like we did here."

Slim paused to reach for a metal mug and pour himself some dark, bitter brew. He looked around at the girls.

"Well, that night passed and they didn't find her, and the next day, and another night."

"What happened to her?" Becky asked. She could picture the frantic search for the lost child.

"Those mustang tracks they found—were they from the black stallion?" Alison asked eagerly.

Slim gulped back his coffee. "I'm gettin' to that. Listen, now. Gretchen woke up with the old mare running alongside a galloping black horse. She tried to stop the mare, but she didn't have a halter or bridle. She couldn't reach the knots to untie herself and jump off, either. They just trotted and galloped along till sundown, when they joined up with a bunch of wild mares.

"The mares greeted the newcomer, and when they discovered those grain sacks, they got excited, not having any grain in their wild life. They started chewing at those grain sacks and nipping at Gretchen's legs until she was screaming in fear and pain.

"That black stallion was there in a bound. He drove off his mares, chewed through the ropes, took Gretchen by the collar and set her on the ground, as gentle as could be."

"Wow!" Alison exclaimed. "Could he really do that?"

"Well, he did. This is a true story I'm telling you, not made up." Slim glared at her again. "Anyway, it was dark by now and the wolves were howling. Gretchen was howling, too, she was so scared, but she finally fell asleep in the grass, and when she woke up, there were no horses in sight. She drank from a stream, ate some berries and stayed where she was, like her pa had told her to do

if she got lost. But no one came, and that night again she fell asleep, crying, with the wolves howling in the valley.

"But the next day, when she woke up, there was that old mare, standing over her sound asleep, with her ears flopped down and her lower lip hanging. Gretchen jumped up and tried to get on the mare's back, but she was too tall. She tried grabbing her by the mane to lead her to a rock she could climb on, but that mare wouldn't budge. Poor Gretchen began to howl and blubber again, she was so hungry and tired and scared.

"While she was standing there sobbing, she heard fast hoofbeats, and when she turned around, there was that coal black stallion, all gleaming and prancing and proud. Gretchen stretched out her arms to him, and that horse grabbed her by the collar of her dress and lifted her right up on the mare's back. Then he must have told that old girl to go home, because by noon, the mare showed up in camp with her empty grain sacks and Gretchen on her back.

"Well, her folks were glad to see her, even though they'd lost their grain. Gretchen showed them the nips on her legs and told them all about the black stallion."

"Is that really true?" Becky said doubtfully.

"Yep. Gretchen lived to be an old old lady and had the scars on her legs till the day she died. Of course, the story of the black stallion didn't end there. Men hunted him and chased him the rest of his life. They captured all his mares, but they could never get him. In the end, like I told Alison, he jumped off a cliff in Rainbow Valley,

rather than be taken. He was one brave horse." Slim shook his head, remembering.

"So he hates men, but if there's a girl in distress he helps them?" Alison asked.

"Seems to be. Although he hasn't been seen much over the years. Maybe there's been no unhappy girl needing his help, till Alison here got charged by that cow moose." Slim reached forward and poured himself another cup of coffee. "You girls want any?"

"No thanks!" Becky spoke for them all. Slim's coffee was made by putting handfuls of coffee grounds straight into boiling water and then letting it boil some more on the fire. It was dark and bitter and thick as cough syrup.

Meg had been thinking. "If it was Diablo who chased off the moose, then it was Diablo Thomas went after," she said with a shiver. "Not a real horse at all."

Alison got up and paced back and forth in front of the fire. "If Diablo likes girls," she said, "it means we're the only ones who can rescue him."

"I wouldn't be too sure of that," Slim said. "If Diablo had to choose between helping a girl or destroying a man, I think his hate might be stronger."

"You're all talking as if this ghost horse was real!" Becky stood up, too. "I'm sorry, Slim, but I think it's just an old story you made up."

Alison faced her cousin across the flames. "I wish you were right. But I've seen it, the ghost. And I saw what it did to Chuck today, and now Rob's gone, too."

They stared at each other.

Slim looked up and the firelight gleamed in his eyes. "I can tell you one thing for sure. It's not just an 'old story.' Gretchen was my grandmother, and I saw them scars on her legs myself."

CHAPTER 20

CROSSING THE CAULDRON

The three girls were thunderstruck. "Your grandmother!" Alison said finally. "She was Gretchen? The girl Diablo rescued?"

"When I was a kid, up north of here," Slim said, "my father would show me Diablo's tracks around our cabin. Diablo's ghost hung around until my grandmother died, back in the sixties.

"How did your dad know they were Diablo's tracks?" Becky asked, still doubting.

Slim sighed. "My dad was with the men who trailed him and finally hounded him to his death, and he knew the tracks." Slim stared at the fire. "I think he was sorry he'd caused the death of that brave animal. A lot of the men were, but it was too late."

"I'm going to check on Windy and Shadow," Becky said. She took a pocket flashlight and walked over to where they'd tethered the horses. Running her hands over Windy's legs, she was glad to find them cool and firm. No swelling or hot spots.

"Good girl," she told Windy. "You rest now and fill your belly with mountain grass."

Shadow whinnied nervously and Becky found her soft nose and held her face against it. "Whatever tomorrow brings, I'll look after you. I'll get you back to Mustang Mountain Ranch, safe and sound," she told the little mare. She wished she felt as sure as she sounded.

A wolf pack had started howling in the next valley. It was the saddest sound in the world, Becky thought. She heard footsteps in the grass. Meg stepped out of the shadows. "Everything all right?"

"The horses seem okay. They've got good grazing for the night, and Shadow's finally settling down."

"The wolves won't frighten her?"

"I hope not—as long as they stay far away. It sounds like they're in the next valley."

Meg sucked in her breath. "That's where I think Thomas must be. Slim's been drawing us a map in the ground. He says Rainbow Valley is on the other side of the river, over the next ridge."

"Don't worry. Thomas knows how to keep the wolves away. It's how *we* get across Cauldron River that worries me," Becky said in a low voice. They could hear the roar of the rapids below. It sounded louder in the darkness.

"And why haven't Rob and Chuck come back?"

Meg shivered. "What if Slim is right, and Diablo has caused all this trouble?"

"I still think this ghost horse talk is crazy," Becky muttered. "But if it's real, we all know the dark force that brought Diablo's ghost back. It's Alison, full of anger and jealousy and bad thoughts."

She could see Meg shake her head in the beam from her pocket light. "Come on, Becky, don't say things like that! We've all got to work together if we're going to find Thomas and get back safely."

Thomas woke up from a dream in which he was terribly thirsty. Waking was slow and painful. First he felt his burning thirst and dry lips. That was real. Then the throbbing pain in his head. That was real, too. He was cold, shivering, and his back ached. There was the smell of horse.

Palouse! Thomas opened his eyes. The tunnel was almost pitch black. The little light that filtered through the gaps in the rock that sealed the entrance was from a fitful moon. But Thomas could see the outline of Palouse standing between him and the tunnel entrance, as if on guard.

He knew with a sickening rush of memory where he was. In the mine. The tunnel had partly collapsed and something had hit him on the head. How long had he been lying here?

He tried to croak Palouse's name. He needed water.

Palouse blew softly, then poked him with his nose. Thomas caught the big head between his hands. "Help me up, Palouse," he whispered. He grabbed his Appaloosa's silvery mane and staggered to his feet.

The sight of the fallen beams and boulders terrified him. In places, there was barely room to stand. He worked his way carefully along Palouse's back, clinging to the saddle, until he reached the saddlebag. There must be one bottle of water left!

✱

Next morning, when the three girls woke up, there was still no sign of Chuck and Rob. It was a dull day. Clouds hung around the mountain peaks like torn banners, and the air was chill. Becky, Alison and Meg had a cold breakfast of fruit bars, worrying the whole time.

"Where *are* they?" Becky looked down at Cauldron River, tearing along between its low banks.

"It most likely got dark while they were looking for Chuck's horse, so they made camp for the night," Slim said. He was sitting cross-legged by the embers of last night's fire, whittling a long stick.

"We should stay here and wait for them," Becky announced, shivering.

"We came to look for Thomas." Alison was rolling up her blanket. "We should go on to Rainbow Valley, like we planned."

"If you hadn't charged ahead with Rob and Chuck, Ms. Rodeo Rider," Becky said angrily, "we'd still all be together.

But since you didn't, we'll have to wait for them."

"What do *you* think, Meg?" Alison wheeled to face her, her hands on her hips.

"I think we should go on." Meg's face was white. Strands of her ponytail hung around her face. She hadn't slept well—they must find Thomas! "We could leave a note for Rob and Chuck ..." she faltered.

"Oh, sure," Becky said sarcastically. "And how would they find a *note* in the middle of the wilderness?" She waved her arms at the expanse of ridge and valley and peaks surrounding them.

Slim worked his bent body into a standing position. "This damp's got into my bones," he grumbled. He held out the long pole that he'd been sharpening while they were arguing. "Any of you got something red? We can attach it to this pole and set it on the top of the ridge. The boys'll spot that."

The three girls stared at him. Why hadn't *they* thought of that?

"That's very smart, Slim," Alison said. She dug into her saddlebag. "Here. Use this." She pulled out a red sock with a blue stripe around the top.

Becky wrote the note on a page torn out of Windy's training log. They stuffed it in the sock and pulled the sock down over the pole stuck into the ground near their firepit. Then the four of them set off down the riverbank, leading the horses.

"I guess I'll ride Shadow," Alison announced. "After all, she *is* our extra horse."

"Bareback, with no bridle?" Meg looked doubtful as she tightened Cody's cinch. "You could ride double with me."

"I hate riding double." Alison tossed her head like a nervous horse. "We'll be fine."

"Are you crazy?" Becky cried. "Shadow's never crossed a river like this in her life! The only water she's even *waded* in is a stagnant waterhole in Wyoming."

"All *right*!" Alison stormed. "I won't ride her until we get to the other side of the river. Quit ganging up on me." She thrust Shadow's lead rope at Becky. "Here, you lead her across."

The truth was, Alison was relieved not to be taking Shadow into the swift-flowing water. She had to summon every sliver of courage to cross Cauldron River herself. The memories of the day before, with Copper being swept off his feet were too fresh.

Slim squinted upstream. "That looks like a safe place to cross." He pointed. "It's wider and not so deep."

"Are you sure?" Alison gulped. This river had almost swallowed Chuck—did they dare trust Slim?

"Just in case," said Slim, "we'll go one by one. Angle upstream. That way, the current won't catch you sideways. I'll go first." He rode Agnes into the water.

They watched him cross safely, the water only up to the mule's belly.

"I'll go next." Becky scowled at her cousin, wishing Alison had not brought Shadow into this danger. She urged Windy into the river, holding Shadow's rope loosely so

she'd have the freedom to choose her own way.

But at the first chill of ice-cold water flowing against her legs, Shadow panicked. She plunged downstream, yanking the rope out of Becky's hand. Becky knew that once Shadow lost her footing in the deep water, she would have no chance. "Get Cody downstream from her," she shrieked at Meg. "Try to turn her head!"

Meg scrambled onto Cody's saddle. They plunged into Cauldron River after the frightened mare. Cody was a strong horse, experienced with icy rivers. He struck out downstream, came level with Shadow and then turned for the opposite shore.

Becky rode Windy up on Shadow's other side, so that she was squeezed between the two horses. She reached for the dangling lead rope but it was torn out of her grasp by the fast current.

From the riverbank, Alison watched in horror. Would they all be swept away? Becky's face was twisted with effort. In that terrifying moment, with the water foaming between Becky and the struggling horse, Alison realized how much Becky loved Shadow. It had nothing to do with the rivalry between them. Becky was even willing to risk her mother's precious Windy to save the little paint mare from the river.

At that moment, Cody gave a great plunge forward. As he did, Meg leaned out and grabbed the rope that was streaming out in the current. "I've got her!" she screamed.

With Cody's sturdy body to lean on and the rope in Meg's hand, Shadow stopped her wild struggle with the

river. Slowly, they worked their way across the rapids to the opposite shore. The three horses pulled themselves up the riverbank.

Meg handed Shadow's lead rope to Becky and slid from Cody's back. "Good work, boy." She hugged his big head. "Good horse."

Slim trotted toward them on Agnes. "Well, you sure did that the hard way," he shouted. "I'll go back for Alison."

He rode his mule across the river to where Alison was sagged in relief on the shore.

"You ready for a little mule ride?" Slim held out his hand to her. They splashed across the shallow ford to the others.

"I'm so glad you're all right," Alison panted, sliding off Agnes's back.

"Shadow almost wasn't!" Becky wouldn't look at her. Her face was set in grim lines as she led Shadow up the gravel bank.

"I won't ride her," Alison called after her cousin. "I'll ride double with Meg, on Cody."

Becky just grunted and tied Shadow's rope back to Windy's saddle.

Leaving the river behind, they rode up the ridge on the other side. From here, they looked into Rainbow Valley at last. The flat gray muskeg bog covered the valley floor, spreading like spilled paint.

"Thomas couldn't cross that!" Becky cried. "He must have gone another way." She remembered only too well when Windy had got stuck in a bog the summer before,

just as she was about to give birth to Breezy. Muskeg bogs could be deadly for horses.

Slim shook his head. "There *is* no other way. Let's go down closer and take a look."

Sure enough, they found Palouse's hoofprints, deep in the bog mud along the edge of the trees. "Looks like Thomas must have rode around," Slim commented. "These tracks are a couple days old. If we stay in his tracks, we should be okay."

But Windy remembered the bog, too. She backed away from the gray mat of muskeg, snorting and pawing the earth. Becky struggled to control her. "She won't go … I'll have to lead her." She untied Shadow's rope from her saddle. A white rim of fear showed around the little mare's eyes.

Becky dismounted and handed Windy's lead rope up to Alison. "Why did you have to bring Shadow?" she yelled. "Look at her—the bog spooks her, too. *Everything* out here spooks her!"

Alison squinted at her cousin, trying not to cry. "All right. It was a mistake to bring her. I'm sorry!"

"We're wasting time," Meg burst out. "If these *are* Palouse's tracks, Thomas might be stuck in the bog. We've got to hurry!"

Becky followed the string, leading a reluctant Shadow. Every once in a while, she paused to bend back a tree branch. She was leaving a trail for Rob, and Chuck, in case they tried to follow them.

CHAPTER 21

HEARTBREAK VALLEY

Hours later, Thomas's trail suddenly ended.

Slim rubbed his bristly beard. "Where'd he go?" he mumbled to himself. "He didn't go on, and he sure didn't go into the bog. He must have headed uphill." He scanned the ground. "Yup, here's his tracks. Looks like he was moving fast, like he was chasing something."

"How could he have the strength?" Becky draped her arms around Shadow's neck. The treacherous trail around the bog had taken its toll on all of them, riders and horses. The horses were sweaty and exhausted. Cody was especially weary, carrying both Alison and Meg.

"Palouse is tough," Meg sighed. She had ridden him on mountain trails through the moonlight the summer before, following Wildfire. "He'd go on as long as Thomas asked."

"Well, *these* horses can't go much farther." Becky wiped her forehead with the sleeve of her shirt. She knew that traveling in the sucking mud along the bog had been twice as hard on the horses as dry ground. "Especially not up that hill." She glanced at the steep incline where Thomas had left his tracks.

"What's on the other side, Slim?" Meg asked.

"That'd be Heartbreak Valley," grunted Slim.

"The place with all those mines!" Becky cried. "Remember? Dad showed us Heartbreak Valley on the map. But why would Thomas go there?"

"Maybe following Diablo?" Meg peered up the ridge. "Let's go."

"We'll take a break first," Slim declared. Meg felt like protesting, but it was no use. They did need to rest.

They walked the horses a short distance up the ridge. On the side of the hill was a small meadow and a spring where they let the horses drink and graze. "Fill up your water bottles. There'll be precious little water or food once we get over in Heartbreak Valley," Slim told them. "For us, or the horses."

They filled their bottles from the spring, then tucked them in their saddlebags. "Do you notice how we're letting Slim make all the decisions?" Becky whispered to Meg. "I mean, sure, he knows the country like the back of his hand, but he's a crazy old cook who believes in ghost horses."

Meg's blue eyes were troubled. "And you don't."

Becky was caught off guard. "No, I don't!" she spluttered. "I mean, not really. It's one thing to tell ghost stories

in front of a fire. It's another to go chasing after ghosts in the wilderness."

"Thomas thinks everything has a spirit—even trees and mountains," Meg said slowly. "I guess I kind of agree with him."

"Oh, for Pete's sake! We have enough *real* things to worry about out here without imaginary spirits." Becky went blustering off. "The altitude's getting to you."

But when they remounted and rode to the top of the hill, it was Slim who hesitated. He sat on Agnes and scanned the rock-strewn landscape. "No sign of the boy." He slumped in his saddle, looking suddenly very old and tired. "Are you girls sure you want to go on?"

"Did Thomas come this way?" Meg asked quickly.

"Well, maybe he did. But I couldn't track him here. The ground's too hard."

"Maybe we could just look—see if he made a fire, or left any trace ..." Meg begged.

Becky had fished binoculars out of her pack and was focusing on the tunnel openings on the far hill. "Are those the old gold mines?" She handed the binoculars to Slim. "Those holes with the heaps of rock?"

Slim waved the binoculars away. "My eyes are as good as ever. Yep, those are the mine tunnels."

Becky was looking through the glasses again. "They don't look very safe any more. Some of them are all caved in."

"They weren't safe in the first place!" Slim exclaimed. "A lot of miners and prospectors left their bones in this valley. How do you think it got its name?"

"Let me see," Meg reached for the glasses. "What if Thomas is in ... one of those tunnels?"

"Don't be silly," Becky said. "How would he get way up there, and why?"

"Can we make up our mind what we're doing?" Alison moaned from behind Meg. "Riding double is no picnic, for me, or poor old Cody. If we're stopping, I'm getting off."

Meg and Becky exchanged glances. "Please," Meg begged, "let's go a bit farther."

Thomas knew his situation was desperate. He had shared his last bottle of water with Palouse the night before. Since early morning, he had been trying to move the rocks that blocked the entrance, but it was no use. He was too weak from the blow to his head, and any exertion made him dizzy.

The daylight outside hurt his eyes. That must also be the bump on my head, he thought. He tried to peer out one of the gaps in the rock, but all he could see was the barren, empty valley. He needed water.

Thomas put his hand on Palouse's forehead and told him to stay still. Slowly and painfully he worked his way toward the back of the tunnel, where he had heard water dripping. If he could find the source, perhaps he and Palouse could stay alive a little longer.

As Becky, Meg, Alison and Slim scrabbled down the rough rocky slopes of Heartbreak Valley, things started to go wrong.

First, Molly threw a shoe.

"We'll have to unpack her load and share it among the other horses," Slim grumbled. It took long minutes to untie Molly's load, repack the supplies and start out with Molly walking behind them.

Then Windy began to limp, just slightly, but enough to make Becky frantic. "Wait, stop!" She slid from her saddle. "She's off balance and stumbling. Something's wrong."

"Maybe it's a stone bruise," Meg said. "These rocks are so sharp."

"That's because they're not natural," Slim grunted disapprovingly. "They've been dynamited and dug up and slid down. It's a terrible place for horses."

"And if it's a stone bruise, it's bound to get worse." Becky's brown eyes were worried. "Let's get out of here."

"Just let me go a little farther—not much, I promise," Meg pleaded.

No one said anything. They were sure that this was useless.

"Becky, stay here with Windy and Shadow," Meg insisted. She pulled back her ponytail tightly, scanning the far valley wall with its dark tunnel openings, desperate for any sign of Thomas. "Alison, you stay, too. Cody's getting really tired carrying us both. I'm going on."

"I can't let you go alone," Old Slim sighed. "We'll go

as far as that dry creek bed. If young Thomas came this way, he might have camped there."

Meg gave him a grateful smile. Alison slipped from Cody's back. It had been a long, uncomfortable ride behind Meg.

Slim gave Agnes a kick and she rattled off down the rocky slope. Meg followed on Cody.

"Don't stay long!" Becky yelled at them. She turned to Alison with fear in her eyes. "I hate this! Now Meg and Slim are heading off alone. We're splitting up again."

"They aren't going far," Alison sighed, rubbing her sore thighs. "We'll be able to see them from here."

CHAPTER 22

DANGER IN THE TUNNEL

Thomas felt along the rock wall till his hand touched wetness. Water was trickling down the wall of the tunnel and dripping into a natural basin at the bottom. He scooped it up with his hand, drank a mouthful. It tasted stale, but cool. Thomas scooped as much water as he could into his hat, to take back to Palouse.

The effort made him dizzy and he was forced to sit, holding his wet hat. From here the tunnel thrust farther into the mountain. It was as black as night.

Thomas staggered back toward Palouse. He had to bend his head in places to keep from hitting it on ceiling beams that had sagged or collapsed. Every once in a while, he heard a tiny skitter of falling earth, like a whisper of danger. Thomas knew that at any second the whole

roof of the tunnel could come crashing down on them. In the meantime, Palouse needed water.

While Palouse dipped his nose into the hat, Thomas tried again to peer through a crack in the rocks at the tunnel's entrance. It was hard to see more than a small section of the valley at a time.

But what was that? Movement? Horses and people on the hill opposite? Two horses. He wanted to shout, but didn't dare. The sound alone could bring down more rock on his head.

Thomas forced his weary, buzzing brain to work. Some way to signal without noise—he needed a signal! Something white or brightly colored that would show up against the black rock. He looked frantically around his narrow prison. The yellow rain slicker tied on Palouse's saddle caught his eye. If only he had the strength to get it off and push it through the crack in the rock. If only they would look up!

Meg and Slim were crossing an old bridge over the dry creek when more bad luck struck. Agnes's right foreleg punched through a rotten board, and the mule fell to her knees. Slim was tossed off.

"OW! Blazes, it's my hip," he roared in pain, holding his right side. He sat up. "And just look at poor old Aggie! She's broken her leg." He squinted his eyes at Meg. "That's it, we're done for. You might as well put a bullet through both our brains."

Meg jumped off Cody and knelt beside Slim. "Don't say that! Do you think your hip is broken?"

"Ow. Nah, it's not broken." Slim flexed his right leg. "Just hurts like blazes. I guess I'm too stringy and tough to break." He tried to grin, but it came out more of a grimace. "Take a look at Agnes. See how bad she is."

Agnes was now standing with her head down, her long ears drooped, her right hoof barely grazing the ground. She let out a loud bray as Meg gently examined her leg. "I can't tell for sure, but I don't think it's broken …" She turned to Slim. He was staring as if he'd seen a ghost. "What's the matter? What are you looking at?"

Slim was pointing with a crooked finger. "Do you see that, up on the ledge? A black horse! It's Diablo. He's the one who did this." Slim turned the air blue with curses.

Meg stared in the direction of his pointing finger. At first she saw nothing, then gasped. "It's not Diablo. It's … yellow. A big bright yellow patch."

"Slim," she screamed, "it might be Thomas! He might be trapped in there and trying to signal. I've got to go!"

From farther up the hillside, Becky and Alison had watched in horror as Agnes stumbled and Slim fell. Now, they could see Meg making frantic arm movements and hear her screams.

"I'm going to see what's wrong." Alison raced off down the hill.

"Wait!" Becky shouted. But Alison was gone, leaving her with all the horses. As fast as she could, Becky tethered Shadow, Molly and Windy, then threw herself down

the hill after her cousin, stumbling over the rough stones. To her amazement, she saw Meg and Alison start off up the other side of the valley at a run. What on earth was happening?

Old Slim was pale with the pain in his hip by the time Becky reached him. He managed a faint grin. "Those two crazy girls have run off," he told her.

"Where are they going?" Becky pressed her hand to Slim's forehead. It was clammy and cold, not a good sign. The whole world started to whirl and Becky knew that at any second she would panic. That was the deadliest danger of all in the wilderness. She forced herself to take deep breaths. "Slim! Why did they go and leave you like this?"

"It's Diablo," Slim groaned. "That black horse, up there. I saw him."

"There's no horse, Slim." Becky struggled to keep from losing control. She looked up to the ledge where Slim was pointing. "There's nothing but a, but a ... yellow rain slicker, hanging out of a tunnel!"

She turned back to Slim. "Listen," she said urgently, "did Alison and Meg see that? Do they think Thomas is in the tunnel?"

"If he is," Slim said slowly, "the black horse put him there and he'll never get out. The tunnel's collapsed."

Becky's head whirled again. "I sh-should go and help them," she stammered, "but I can't just leave you." She put her hand behind his neck. "Can you ride Agnes?"

"Don't think I can." Slim shook his head. "Poor old mule's hurt worse than I am."

Becky made a quick inspection of Agnes's injured leg. "She can walk," she announced. "Do you think, if I helped you, you could get on Cody?"

"It's a darn sight better than lyin' here on this hard, stony ground." Slim reached for her arm and tried to stand. As she helped him up, Becky was surprised at how heavy the old man was. She could see how the pain in Slim's hip drained the strength right out of him. They struggled to get him up on Cody's back, but once he was settled in the saddle, he looked better, and some of the color came back into his face.

"That's good," she panted. "I'll take you up to where the horses are tied and get you comfortable."

"C'mon, Agnes," Slim called. "We're gettin' out of this wretched valley. And none too soon, if you ask me!"

As they started up the hill, Becky looked at Alison and Meg, now climbing the narrow ledge to the tunnel opening. How she wished she was with them! She cupped her hands around her mouth and bellowed with all her might, "I'll be back! Be careful."

Meg heard Becky shout, but couldn't make out what she said. It didn't matter. Nothing was going to stop her getting to Thomas. She was sure the yellow raincoat was his signal.

"OOOH! I hate heights." Alison clung to the mountainside as they edged their way up the ledge.

"Don't look down," Meg said urgently. "We're almost

there." She kept her eyes fixed on the raincoat dangling above them.

At last they reached the blocked tunnel. Meg peered through a crack between the boulders. "Thomas," she cried. "Thomas, it's Meg!"

She heard Palouse's low whinny and a faint voice from the other side of the rock barrier. "Meg. I hoped it was you." Thomas's voice got a little louder as he crawled closer to the entrance. "There was a cave-in. I hurt my head. I can't move the rocks."

Meg could hear the pain in his voice. She forced hers to be steady. "Don't worry. We'll get you out." Alison joined her, and they heaved at the boulders with all their strength, first one, then another, until their fingernails were broken and their hands were grazed and bleeding.

"These stupid rocks ... won't move!" Alison groaned almost an hour later. "They're wedged too tight against one another."

"It's no use." Thomas's voice was fading.

"We'll have to go for help." Alison tugged at Meg's sleeve. "Come on."

"I can't just leave Thomas alone in there." Meg turned a stricken face to her. "What if there's another cave-in? Let's keep trying!" She pounded at the rocks in desperation.

CHAPTER 23

BECKY MAKES DECISIONS

Striding beside Cody up the rocky slope to the other horses, Becky remembered the spring where they'd rested the horses, on the other side of the ridge.

"Hang on, Slim," she told him. "I'll just get the horses, and we'll go camp by the spring where we rested before." She collected Windy, Shadow and Molly from where she'd tethered them. Shadow stamped and rolled her eyes, looking anxiously around, as if ready to bolt. "I know." Becky stroked her cream and brown side. "You don't understand any of this. You just wish you were back in Wyoming—no trees, lots of open spaces. I wish I were there, too. Anywhere but here!"

Becky fought down the waves of fear and anger that swept over her. She knew they could not afford another

mistake. No more stumbles, no more falls. She was angry at Alison for racing off and leaving her alone with Slim and all the horses. Angry at Rob for taking off with Chuck and at Thomas for chasing after wild horses. What was the use? They'd all done one stupid thing or another. "The important thing," she whispered to Shadow, "is to stop and think before every move from now on—no matter how slow that makes us." Once they got away from this awful valley, it would be better.

They crested the ridge and made their way down through the trees to the resting spot. "Let me help you off Cody," Becky told Slim.

Slim just nodded, too miserable to talk, and leaned his full weight on her as she helped him out of the saddle. She made him as comfortable as possible, stretched out on a pad of bedrolls.

"I'll make a nice smoky fire," Becky said. "Fires get noticed in this country—someone may see it from the air and fly closer to investigate."

She looked up at the sky. It was hard to tell whether a plane could spot smoke through the thick cloud cover, but it would give her something to do. She glanced at her watch—nearly three o'clock already. As she gathered wood for the fire, Becky found herself thinking about Rob, hoping he was all right.

"Slim?" she asked, once the fire was burning. "Why do you think Rob and Chuck didn't make it back to our camp last night?"

He didn't answer right away, just groaned and tried to

make himself more comfortable. Then he said, "I guess there's only one answer to that. They were lookin' for Chuck's horse, and they didn't want to give up before dark."

"You think Copper drowned?"

"I didn't want to say it." Slim nodded. "But Cauldron River got its name because the rapids end in a big round rock pool where they swirl around and then disappear underground."

"Like a sinkhole!" Becky exclaimed.

"That's right. And if Copper got swept down the river into that, not even his bones will be found."

Becky sprang to her feet and paced back and forth. "What if Chuck and Rob went into the sinkhole to save Copper? Chuck is crazy about that horse!"

"Take my advice. Don't think the worst." Slim shook his head. "The two of them are probably on their way back to the ranch right now." He shifted position to get closer to the fire. "I'll tell you what. I'll put green branches on the fire to make smoke for a signal. You take Cody and go look for those two girls, and Thomas. They're the ones you should be worried about."

"Go back to the mines?" Becky stared down at him. "I can't just leave you here by yourself."

"What do ya think? I'm going to blow away?" Slim fanned away the smoke that was drifting toward his eyes. "Go on, now. You're making me nervous, pacing like that."

"If you're sure you're all right, maybe I should."

Becky was trying to think clearly. "I can leave food where you can reach it, and firewood ..."

"That's it. You get goin'. But be real careful. One day, the whole danged mountain is going to cave in, it's so full of holes. Thomas was crazy to go in there, but I suppose Diablo led him straight to it."

I wish he wouldn't talk like that, Becky thought. One minute he sounds okay, and the next he's talking wild. "You stay right here and watch the horses for me," she told him. "Don't *you* dare disappear!" She filled water bottles from the spring and tied them to Cody's saddle.

"I'm not likely to be goin' anywhere, with me and Agnes being lame," Slim said. "You better skedaddle."

Becky tied the horses and Agnes close together in a patch of good grass near the spring. She checked Windy over and the mare seemed fine. It was Shadow who still started at every noise, and quivered if a pine branch brushed her flank. "You'll be fine," Becky told her. Shadow's ears came forward as if she were paying attention. Becky cupped her soft nose in her hand. "I'll be back as soon as I can."

She turned and waved to Slim as she rode Cody back up the ridge to Heartbreak Valley. She hoped she was doing the right thing. She felt very alone.

Thomas's voice came faintly through the boulders to Meg and Alison. "There might be another way in. I can feel a breeze at the back of the tunnel, and the air smells fresh."

"He's right." Meg shut her eyes and leaned against the rock she'd been trying unsuccessfully to move. "Some of these tunnels might be connected."

Alison grabbed her hand. "So what are we waiting here for? Let's see if we can find another entrance that's not blocked."

Taking a deep breath, Alison edged her way around the rampart of rock at the end of the narrow ledge.

"C'mon, Meg. It's not so bad." She reached back to help Meg around the jutting rock. Beyond, a wider track zigzagged up the mountainside. The first tunnel mouth they came to was a dead end—shallow and not supported by timbers. Alison muttered as they squirmed back out into the light. "Ugh, I hate small dark places like that."

Meg squeezed her hand. "But you went in anyway. Thanks."

"Don't say thanks!" Alison snatched her hand away. "This is all my fault."

"What are you talking about?"

"I sent Thomas after Diablo," Alison confessed. "I told him there was a magnificent black stallion in Rainbow Valley, and he believed me. I told him that *before* I got charged by the moose."

"You sent him after a ghost horse! Why?" Meg's face fell. "Why would you do that?"

"Oh, I was jealous, and I didn't want you to have fun. And I didn't really believe in Diablo then," Alison said in a low voice. "I'm so sorry, Meg." Tears were spilling

down her cheeks. "That's why we have to get Thomas out of there. I'll never forgive myself if anything happens to him."

Meg clutched her hand again. "Come on. We have to go higher." She threw back her head and looked up the cliff face. "There's a bigger tunnel up there."

CHAPTER 24

MEG'S CHOICE

"Have you got a flashlight?" Meg peered into the black mouth of the higher tunnel.

Alison felt in her jacket pocket. "Just this little one." She pulled out a flashlight the size of a fat pen. "I don't know how long it will last."

They stepped into the tunnel, their feet crunching on the rocks. "How do we know *this* tunnel connects with Thomas's?" Alison's voice echoed weirdly around them.

"We don't," Meg muttered. "We'll have to keep trying until we find one that does."

"I can't believe they thought they'd find something as beautiful as gold in such a dark, dirty, disgusting place." Alison's thin flashlight beam bounced around the rough rock walls. "I wonder if there's any gold left?"

They crunched deeper into the mine. The tunnel twisted and turned. "Alison, stop!" Meg suddenly reached out and grabbed Alison's arm. "What's that in front of you?"

Alison swung the light down. Then she slowly sank to her knees. Another step and she would have walked into a square hole. "Thanks," she said shakily. "That'll teach me to look for gold, instead of where I'm going!"

"Shine your light down there," Meg urged.

The light showed that the well, or whatever it was, seemed to have no bottom. Alison shuddered. "If I'd fallen down that, it would have been the end of me."

"Look." Meg pointed. "There are rungs built into the side. It's some kind of shaft. Maybe it connects with Thomas's tunnel below."

"Are you suggesting we climb down there?" Alison's voice rose to a screech. "Meg, I can't. It's small and closed in *and* deep—everything I hate!"

"Stay here then, but give me the light."

"No, I can't stay in the dark. You go first, and guide my feet."

Meg started down. Alison put the flashlight between her teeth and followed Meg into the shaft.

They seemed to go down forever, rung after rung. Their sore hands burned on the rough iron bars.

Then Meg stopped. "Oh, help!"

"Whazza madder?" Alison mumbled between her clenched teeth.

"There's a rung missing." Meg's voice was shaking.

"And the one below doesn't feel very solid. Alison, I don't think we can go any farther. I feel like I'm going to fall!"

Alison held the rung above her with one hand, took the flashlight out of her mouth and shone it straight down. "Hang on. The bottom's not too far down. You can let go." She held the light until she heard Meg thump to the ground.

At the same time there was a low rumble in the tunnel. "What's that?" Alison hissed.

"I don't know," Meg called up to her, "but I don't like it. Hurry."

Alison put the flashlight back between her teeth, swung past the missing rung and let herself drop.

They hurried along the tunnel, which turned first one way, then another. They could hear water dripping, smell dust. "What's that?" A sound froze them to the spot. It came again—the low, unmistakable snorting of a horse.

"It's Palouse. Look!" The flashlight showed large wood beams lying at crazy angles, a chaos of rock and rotting wood. "Thomas—are you here?" Meg called.

"Not so loud," they heard a voice. "I think shouting could cause another cave-in. I'm here, by Palouse."

The tall Appaloosa looked like a pale ghost in that terrible place, but Meg and Alison had never been so glad to see a horse in their lives. Thomas was sitting near him, propped against the wall.

"We found a shaft," Alison told him. "It connects to this tunnel from another one, higher up."

Meg crouched beside Thomas. She found his hand and squeezed it with all her might. Relief washed over her. "Come on, let's get out of here."

"Could Palouse climb this shaft you found?" Thomas asked quietly.

"No, it's like a ladder in a narrow well ..." Meg stopped, realizing what he meant. "No, a horse couldn't get out that way. But we can ... and go for help."

"I can't leave Palouse." Thomas slowly shook his head.

"Thomas!" Meg urged. "There might be another cave-in any second."

"Hush." He smoothed her hair. "I got Palouse into this, and he trusts me. You go and get help. It's all right."

Meg could see his face in the dim light from the cracks in the entrance. There were deep grooves beside his mouth and his dark brown eyes were steady. There was no way she could change his mind. "Alison," she said over her shoulder, "you'll have to go for help by yourself. I'm staying with Thomas."

"Oh, this is ridiculous." Alison shone her flashlight on Meg and Thomas. "I'm not leaving the two of you here to die together, with Thomas's horse! What if the whole roof comes down? What if ..." She could see by the look on Meg's face that there was absolutely no use arguing.

"She's right." Thomas squeezed Meg's hand. "You cannot stay here. It's too dangerous. Go with Alison. Please."

"I'm sorry," Meg said softly. "Just like you can't leave Palouse, I can't leave you."

"You two are both idiots!" Alison muttered hoarsely. "We go to all the bother of finding another tunnel and risk our necks climbing down some rotten old ladder, and now you won't leave." She turned on her heel and stumbled off through the rubble. "It's the stupidest thing I ever heard."

"Alison?" Meg called softly. "I know you can do it. Please hurry."

CHAPTER 25

Cave-in!

Meg and Thomas listened to Alison's footsteps fading away. They watched her light blink out as she turned a corner.

Meg huddled close to Thomas and he put his arm around her. "You shouldn't have stayed," he said.

"Are you hurt?" Meg was suddenly conscious that Thomas was sitting very still.

"I have a lump on my head, and for a while I wasn't sure where I was. Now I can think more clearly, and my head doesn't feel like a swollen watermelon."

"It sounds like you have a concussion!" Meg cried.

"Yes, I think so," Thomas agreed. "There was a kind of explosion ... rocks fell." He sat up straighter and put

his hand to his forehead. "There was a horse! It's coming back to me."

"Tell me about it," Meg urged. "Tell me how you got here!"

So Thomas told her about chasing the black horse, and how the horse had reared up in the mine opening, striking at the beams. "It seemed almost as though he meant to start the cave-in." Thomas shook his head. "But that's impossible. It must have been a dream."

"Maybe not." Meg told him Slim's story of Diablo and why he hated men. "It sounds so real the way Slim tells it," she went on. "He says he saw those scars on his grandmother's legs. And there's something else. Alison was talking about the ghost horse, not a real horse, when she told you that people had seen a wild stallion in Rainbow Valley. Slim told *her* that Diablo had been spotted recently."

"But why would Alison ..." Thomas's voice was low, disbelieving.

"She's been having a bad time. She doesn't want to show it, but she's hurt and mad that her dad didn't take her to Paris. Now she's back here, where she knows no one really wants her ..." Meg paused. "It's no excuse for what she did, but she's really sorry ..."

"And she's Alison," Thomas sighed. "I should have known to ask more questions and not go chasing off after a rumor. I've never heard that legend about Diablo, or I might have been more suspicious."

They were quiet for a long moment. Then Thomas

said, "Meg, I'm glad you're here, but I think you should go. It will be a long time before help comes, tomorrow at the earliest."

Meg put her arms around his waist. "Meanwhile, we're together. That's all that matters to me."

"You shouldn't talk like that," Thomas said shakily, pulling away from her.

Meg felt the sting of his rejection. "Don't you want to be with me?"

"Oh, Meg." He rested his head against hers. "My beautiful Meg. I have been thinking about being with you ever since you went away a year ago."

Meg put her hand against his face. His beard was rough, and his skin felt hot. "You only make sense when you're delirious." She laughed softly. "Why do you only talk like this when you have a fever or a bump on the head?"

"I can't tell you how I feel because you're too young!" Thomas said harshly. "You're fifteen years old. You live in a city on the other side of the continent. When I saw you at the Stampede, I knew how hopeless it was. All I can do is hurt you, talking like this."

Meg could see the pain in his face in the faint light filtering into the tunnel. "Listen to me, Thomas Horne," she said. "I'm not going to be fifteen forever. And maybe I live in the east, but I don't belong there. As soon as I can, I'm going to live here, with Patch, in the west, in the mountains. I can come to college out here—"

"But you might change," Thomas interrupted.

"I haven't changed since last year," Meg reminded him. "How about you? Do you think you'll change?"

"In some ways." Thomas took a deep breath. "But not in the way I feel about you."

Just then, another rumble sounded somewhere over their heads and dirt sifted down on them.

Thomas stiffened. "It's been doing that for hours. I think more of the roof is going to come down."

"Let's move." Meg scrambled to her feet. "Let's try to get away from the entrance."

She held out her hand and helped Thomas to his feet. She could tell he was still woozy because he pulled her close and kissed her very firmly on the lips. She kissed him back.

This was the moment Meg had been waiting for. She clung to Thomas, wishing with all her might that they were anywhere else but this dark, fearful place!

*

Meg's words echoed in Alison's brain as she scrambled back to the shaft. *I know you can do it.* Doesn't she know I'm a walking disaster? Alison thought. I can't do anything right.

Mentally, Alison listed her most recent failures: I messed up in dressage and because of that they sold Duchess, my beautiful horse; I caused a terrible fight between my parents—they're probably going to split up; I lied to Thomas and now he and Meg are trapped in this mine; Chuck's lost his horse; Becky hates me. The only

thing I've done right is adopt Shadow and Patch. And even then I neglected Shadow this year because I was so miserable about moving to Horner Creek.

The rumbled warning of shifting rock made her stop and hold her breath. Hurry! She must hurry.

Back at the shaft, she stopped. With the ladder broken at the bottom, how was she going to reach the rungs? Luckily, she thought, despite being a total disaster as a person, I *am* strong and athletic.

Once more, she clamped the flashlight between her teeth. Wedging her body into the square opening, with her feet against one side and her back against the other, she inched upward, the way she'd seen rock climbers go up a rock chimney.

There! She lunged for the rung above her head and gripped it hard. It held.

Now she was on the ladder. It was hard work, even harder than going down. There was another rumble, and the whole shaft shook. Alison hung on with all her strength. "Oh please," she whispered frantically, "please don't let me die by myself in this shaft—don't let me fall."

The rumbling lessened and she went on climbing. Reaching the top, she shone her light down the tunnel and headed for the entrance. A few more turns and she'd be out in the open air again.

But now the rumbling was a roar beneath Alison's feet. The tunnel under her was caving in. She threw herself on the ground and covered her head with folded arms. She could feel the earth shake under her body and

pictured rocks falling on Meg and Thomas and Palouse.

"No, oh no, oh no!" Alison sobbed, twisting her body, trying to blank out the terrible pictures in her mind. Waves of grief washed over her. She had failed again.

CHAPTER 26

BRAVE HORSE

Riding up the valley toward the tunnel mouth, Becky heard the rumble of falling rock, felt the earth shake.

She threw herself off Cody's back. From the tunnel entrance above, dust was flying. She saw Thomas's yellow raincoat fall and get buried. Then silence.

Becky scrambled partway up the cliff toward the pile of rubble. Thomas was in there! Maybe Meg and Alison, too! She must reach them!

"Alison! Meg!" she shouted into the ringing silence. No answer. She called their names over and over until she was hoarse. The valley mocked her with echoes of her own voice—Alisonnn—Megggg—fading away.

Panic rose in Becky's throat. There was nothing she could do! It was no good trying to batter at all that rock

with her bare hands. Forcing herself to breathe, fighting back the urge to scream and cry and shriek at the sky, Becky slid down the slope and jumped on Cody. "Let's get back to Slim! We need to find help."

The big bay needed no urging. Every instinct told him to run from this place of shifting earth and fearful sound. He lumbered across the valley floor, up the ridge and down the other side to the spring.

Slim was waiting, half sitting, holding his sore hip. He had heard the rumble of the cave-in.

"I couldn't see them, Slim." Becky jumped off Cody's back. "I couldn't see Meg and Alison. I think they're buried in the mine tunnels." She shook her head back and forth, trying to breathe. "I'll have to go for help—ride to the ranch as fast as I can."

She shuddered. "Cody's so slow, but I can't risk Windy. She might go completely lame on me."

"What about your little paint, there?" Slim's calm voice beat back the panic in Becky. "Seems she goes pretty well."

"Shadow?" Becky stared at him. "She's never been ridden that far. It must be nearly fifteen miles to the ranch. Besides, she's totally spooked. I'd never get her across Cauldron River!"

"I've been thinking about that. Look here." Slim grabbed a stick and scratched a map in the dirt. "I figure you can cut a couple of hours off your ride." He showed her on the map. "Don't go back the way we came, crossing the river and all." He drew another line. "If you turn west in Rainbow Valley and go out the narrow end, you'll

wind up at Cowpunch Creek. It's a short ride to Mustang Mountain from there."

"But Alison said that entrance to the valley was blocked with deadfall."

"You might be able to get through." Slim looked up at her. "The young paint is pretty strong and she's got that mustang shuffle. She can cover a lot of ground in a hurry—that's what you need right now."

"You're right," Becky gasped. "Shadow can do it. She has to." She undid Cody's cinch and pulled the saddle off the big horse. A numbing calm had replaced the shaking. She had to hurry, but do everything right. Saddling and bridling Shadow was a familiar routine, checking the position of the saddle, tightening the cinch, checking the stirrups.

"You're going to get us back to the ranch," she whispered to Shadow. "No time for spooking now. We're going to fly."

Alison didn't know how long she lay in that tunnel, hands pressed to her eyes. She never wanted to get up or move again. Time flowed around her. It could have been minutes or hours later that she heard hoofbeats.

Soft, thudding hoofbeats, like the beating of her heart. She raised her eyes and saw in the dim light a kind of black mist in the shape of a prancing horse. Was she dreaming? The horse shape faded, came forward, faded again, almost beckoning her to follow.

Alison was afraid. She remembered how following the black horse had led to disaster. But she also had an image of a huge whirling energy force coming between her and the charging moose. Saving her life. Which was this? The brave rescuing horse, or the avenging Diablo, full of hate for the men who had taken his freedom and life?

I have to try, Alison thought. She fumbled in her pocket for the flashlight, found it and switched it on. The light seemed dimmer—were her batteries running out? Shivering, she got to her feet and followed the sound of the hoofbeats along the tunnel, past the shaft in the floor, into the darkness.

They seemed to draw her on forever, twisting and turning, deeper into the mountain. They turned a sharp corner and suddenly Alison felt the floor slope downward. It was some kind of ramp with a metal track in the middle.

Where were they going? Sometimes the hoofbeats would fade out and then return, as if the horse had got too far ahead and had to circle back to make sure she was coming.

Another corner. The sloping tunnel leveled out and was flat again. There was rock dust in the air, and the smell of damp.

And then there were no more hoofbeats. Alison stopped. Her heart was thudding madly, but as hard as she listened, there was no other sound. She switched off her light to save batteries. No use going on without a guide. The dark closed around her like a smothering

blanket. Never had she felt so abandoned, so helpless. She sank to her knees and let out a howl of despair. "Come back!"

"Hellooo …"

Was that an echo? Astonished, Alison scrambled to her feet and switched her light back on.

"Who's there?" she shouted.

Becky fished for the compass in her saddlebag. Without the sun to guide her on this overcast day, she wanted to be sure she was heading for the ranch.

She and Shadow had been traveling for half an hour at a slow jog. They had ridden down from the spring and headed west. According to her watch, it was five o'clock. She had at least four more hours of good daylight.

Becky tried to remember everything Rob had told her when they were training Shadow back at Horner Creek. She could almost hear his voice in her ear. "Horses are followers. Get Shadow to trust you by acting as her leader."

Thinking about Rob, checking the time and direction, helped Becky drive off her fear, at least for the moment. But what would happen when she rode Shadow into the narrow streambed at the end of Rainbow Valley? Where Shadow would face not just running water but deadfall in her path? Both those things had spooked her badly.

In the back of Becky's mind was her old terror of an

out-of-control horse, rearing, throwing her off, stabbing at her with flashing hooves. It was a fear she had conquered, training Shadow, but now it gripped her once more, like an eagle's talon clutching at her shoulder.

Don't think about it, she gave herself a shake. Pretend you and Shadow are in an endurance race. If this were a real race, she thought, there would be flags marking the trail and a crew of friends with special feed for Shadow and food and drink for me at rest stops. Instead, she was totally alone, somewhere in Rainbow Valley, with a long way to go. She and Shadow were two tiny specks in a vast sweep of wilderness.

"Come on, Shadow. Let's go, girl." She spoke out loud just to hear a human sound. Shadow lengthened out into a fast lope. It was almost as if she understood how important it was to reach the ranch, Becky thought. She wanted to gallop but Becky held her back. She mustn't get too exhausted. Otherwise she'd never make it through that gully at the end of the valley, with its tangle of fallen trees. "Steady, Shadow," Becky soothed.

Shadow had been born on the open range and spent her life on the move with the wild horse herd, but this was different—a long hard ride with someone on her back. Becky knew that her own fear and tension could waste Shadow's precious energy. Stay balanced, Becky told herself. Relax, go with the rhythm of her motion.

Shadow felt her rider relax and slowed to the gait Slim had called the mustang shuffle. It was a jog with almost no bounce that didn't tire her or Becky. And it was

faster than it looked. They were covering the flat valley floor in good time.

Two hours later they reached the place where Rainbow Valley narrowed to a steep ravine with a small stream running through it.

"Okay, Shadow. This is it." Becky got off, looped the reins over her saddle horn and grabbed the lead rope attached to Shadow's halter. She didn't want to be yanking on the mare's mouth if she lost her footing.

They started downstream. Shadow balked at the tangle of fallen trunks and the swift flowing water, but took hesitant steps forward. When they reached a trunk as high as her knees, with the stream gurgling beneath it, she planted her feet and stopped completely.

"Come on!" Becky urged.

But Shadow flattened her ears and tossed her head. Again, Becky saw the white rim of fear around the mare's eyes. She glanced at the steep sides of the gully. "There's no way around, Shadow," she whispered. "We have to go forward."

Shadow whinnied, the sound sudden and startling in the silence. Becky jumped. "I can't do this," she whispered. Then an image of Meg, Alison and Thomas behind a wall of rubble filled her mind. She sucked in her breath and tugged firmly on Shadow's halter. "We have to do this," she said in as stern a voice as she could manage. "Be brave, Shadow, I won't let you get hurt." She pulled branches out of the mare's way and stayed close by Shadow's head, coaxing her to lift first one leg and then

the other over the fallen tree trunk. "That's good—you're almost there!" Shadow whinnied again, as if summoning all her courage.

Becky hugged her hard when she finally cleared the trunk and splashed down the stony streambed toward Cowpunch Creek. "You're the bravest horse that ever was!" she whispered.

The little mustang mare was sweaty and a bit scratched up, but she shook her mane as if to say, "What next?

*

Back in the tunnel, Alison heard Meg's voice. "Alison, is that you?"

"Where are you?" Alison started running, turned a corner of the tunnel.

"We're here. We can see your light!"

"You're all right? You're alive?" Alison thought her heart would burst. Was this another trick of the darkness, a dream? No, she could see them in the pencil of light that bobbed up and down as she ran. Meg and Thomas and Palouse. Meg was running to meet her.

"Alison!" Meg grabbed her and hugged her with all her might, laughing and crying at the same time. "We thought we were trapped. We couldn't find the shaft we came down. Anyway, Thomas wouldn't go, but I was going to try to climb up and find you. Oh! But you found us."

"I had help …" Alison choked, unable to describe the

ghost horse leading her along the dark tunnels. "I thought you two were dead. What happened?"

They were walking back to Thomas, still clinging to each other. "Thomas and I felt the roof was going to come down," Meg explained, "so we moved Palouse farther into the tunnel—just in time."

Thomas was standing beside Palouse, his arm around his horse's neck. He held out his other hand to Alison. "Thank you," he said simply. "You're a good friend to come back for us."

"We … we've got to hurry," she gulped. "My flashlight's almost dead."

"I can't leave Palouse—" Thomas started to say.

"It's all right. There's a ramp that leads to the upper tunnel. It's this way." Alison started down the tunnel.

They hurried after her, Palouse following close behind Thomas. His hoofbeats were loud and ringing on the rock floor. Nothing, Alison realized, like the soft hoofbeats of her ghost horse.

On the last dash for the ranch, Becky let Shadow stretch out into a gallop along Cowpunch Creek. After all the lectures I gave Alison about not pushing Shadow too hard, she thought despairingly, here I am asking her to run her heart out for me!

If they could get there in time, it would still be light enough to send a helicopter. There was still hope.

CHAPTER 27

DIABLO

Alison's flashlight blinked out at the top of the ramp. They were left in a darkness as thick as dense black felt. They couldn't see each other or the tunnel ahead. Alison knew that one wrong turn and they could be hopelessly lost. She put out her hand and found the tunnel wall. "I think we turn left here," her voice echoed in the darkness. "Then we follow that tunnel to the entrance." She wished she was as sure as she tried to sound.

They felt their way along the walls.

Alison had a sudden awful thought. "Stop!" she called. "I forgot. There's still that shaft opening in the floor somewhere between here and the entrance." Her voice quavered. "We'll have to go slow and feel with our feet, or one of us will fall down it."

"Let Palouse be our eyes," Thomas urged. "Even if he can't see the hole, he'll sense it and let us know."

They lined up behind Palouse. Thomas gave a cluck and the gelding moved forward. They followed, holding hands.

After a long time, Palouse stopped and snorted. Alison got down on her hands and knees and felt the floor in the blackness.

"I can feel the corner of the hole," she said at last. "It's about as big as a small desk. There's room for Palouse to get past on the right. I'll stay here till you're all on the other side."

Thomas led the protesting Palouse. Meg followed. Alison crept after them, feeling for the edge of the hole until it was safe to stand up.

"That's it," she called out. "Only a few more turns of the tunnel and we're out of here!"

They went on.

"Is it my imagination, or is it already getting lighter?" Meg strained her eyes in the dark.

At that moment, there was an explosion of noise ahead of them.

They began to run, blundering in the dim light behind Palouse.

As they turned the last corner of the tunnel, Alison screamed, "Diablo, NO!"

A figure was outlined against light from the tunnel mouth, his arms thrown up to protect himself from the slashing hooves of a giant horse. The horse reared above

him, a black whirling fury, striking at the beams of the tunnel entrance.

Palouse whinnied in fear. Thomas struggled to control him. "Watch out!" he shouted. "That's how he started the other cave-in!"

Alison was running, racing down the tunnel with one thought in her mind. Something had infuriated Diablo. She threw herself between the cowering figure and the rearing frenzy of black rage. "Diablo, it's me!" she screamed. "Stop. You don't want to hurt me or my friends."

The shape backed away, whirling into an indistinct mass of light. It spun like a raging stallion turning on an enemy in a fight. But instead of attacking, it leaped out of the tunnel mouth into space—like a horse leaping from a high cliff to its death.

All that was left was the soft light of early evening and a figure crouching against the tunnel wall.

Alison bent down and touched his red hair. "It's Chuck!" she shouted to Meg and Thomas. Then, to Chuck, she soothed, "It's all right—the horse is gone."

Chuck clung to Alison's arm as they zigzagged down the cliff path. Meg and Thomas followed more slowly, with Palouse clopping patiently behind. Sure-footed and unafraid, he had made his way around the rampart of rock with a little help.

"*Was* it a horse—that thing that tried to kill me?" Chuck gasped.

"The ghost of Diablo." Alison nodded, looking back up the cliff face that was now growing darker. "At least, I'm pretty sure."

"But he stopped when you shouted to him," Chuck marveled. "How? Why?"

"He also helped me find Meg and Thomas," Alison murmured. "I'll tell you the whole story later. First, tell *me*—how did you get here?"

"After Rob and I gave up looking for Copper ..." Chuck gulped and began again. "We came back to look for you. We saw your note and found Slim's ford across the river."

He paused again and Alison knew he must be thinking about how he'd made a terrible mistake plunging into Cauldron River at the wrong spot. She squeezed his arm.

"Then what?" Alison urged. "How did you track us after the river?"

Chuck turned to her. "We followed the branches Becky broke along your trail until we spotted the smoke from Slim's fire. Slim told us about the mine tunnels and the cave-in. We agreed that Rob should stay with him, and I should come on to look for you, and Thomas and Meg."

"I'm glad you did." Alison gave Chuck's arm another squeeze. "And I'm really, really sorry about Copper." Once again, a wave of guilt swept over Alison. All of this had been her fault. She was so sorry. She glanced at Chuck's profile. He didn't look so bad, in this light, and when he wasn't trying to be funny.

*

The helicopter hovered like a giant bird over Heartbreak Valley.

"Don't see anything." The pilot circled higher. "I might as well check out the smoke on the other side of the ridge. You say that's your fire?" he shouted back to Becky.

Becky was clutching her mother's hand. "Yes." She nodded.

Laurie and Dan had come with her in the copter, Laurie with first aid supplies for the horses, Dan with picks and shovels.

They circled over the spring.

"There they are!" Becky screamed. "There they *all* are—Alison and Meg and Thomas and Slim and ..." She peered through the smoke at the group waving wildly up at them. "I think it's Chuck and Rob!" She squeezed her mother's hand more tightly. "They made it!"

"Looks like we don't need the search." Dan shared a grin with the pilot. "But I understand Old Slim's hurt pretty bad, and the rest of them have likely had their fill of the wilderness. I'd like you to take them all back to the ranch. Laurie and I will stay here and look after the horses. They may need treatment and rest before they're ready to walk back."

CHAPTER 28

ALISON'S GIFT

"Alison's been awfully quiet," Meg remarked to Becky. "I've hardly spoken to her since we got back." They were stretched out on their bunks, two days after their rescue from Heartbreak Valley.

"It's not like her," Becky agreed. "I wonder what she's plotting ..."

"Becky!" Meg sat up and yanked on her ponytail. "Why does it have to be a plot! Isn't it possible she really feels bad about Diablo and losing Copper, and everything?"

Becky's face flushed and she glared at Meg. "Have you ever known my cousin to admit she was wrong?"

"You're cousins, all right!" was all Meg would say. It was amazing how sometimes Becky and Alison did look

like each other, even though Becky was so fair, and Alison so dark. It was something about that stubborn look in their eyes and the way they set their mouths in a straight line.

Becky was quiet for a moment and then spoke again. "I'll try to believe she's sorry. If anything was going to change Alison, it would be the last few days. I'll never forget how I felt when I thought all of you were trapped inside that mine tunnel and there was nothing I could do to help!"

"But you did!" Meg grinned. "You and Shadow rode like mad to get help. *I'll* never forget my first sight of that helicopter!" She turned and snuggled into her pillow. "It's so nice to be back in a safe warm bunk at Mustang Mountain—I wish I never had to leave!"

"When do you think your parents will be back with the horses?" Rob asked Becky that night.

The two of them were washing dishes after a late dinner. Since getting back to the ranch, they had divided Slim's kitchen duties—Alison, Chuck and Meg cooked, Rob and Becky cleaned up. Slim and Thomas were settled on couches in the dining room, fussed over by all of them. They were both recovering well.

"Mom and Dad will show up when Mom decides the horses are fit to travel," Becky sighed. "I hope Windy is all right." She paused and smiled at Rob. "Now I understand why Mom gets so excited about endurance racing. I

felt it riding Shadow that last stretch—like we were real partners. Wow, she's a great horse."

She stood, musing, with the wet scrub brush dangling from her hand. "If Shadow were mine, I'd train her for the Tevis Cup—the biggest endurance race of them all, from Nevada to California. I'll bet she'd win, too!"

"She might." Rob took the brush out of her hand and nudged her aside. "Here—it's my turn to scrub pots. What I like about endurance races," he went on, "is that there's no big money prizes. People just do it because they love it, and their horses love it." He finished washing a large frying pan and handed it to her. "I guess you're not scared of Shadow anymore."

Becky felt her heart turn to bubbles like the soap in the sink when he smiled like that. "I could never be scared of Shadow! I wish—" She suddenly froze. "Was that the phone?" The radio-phone hardly ever rang, and it was always something important when it did.

Becky dropped the pan and tore to the office to find Alison already speaking into the radio-phone in a low voice.

"Uh-huh ... yes, okay," Alison said. There was a long pause. "I don't care, whatever you ... okay ... the line's breaking up. Okay, bye." She slammed down the phone and, without a word, ran out of the office across the dining room and out the screen door.

"What was that?" Chuck asked, staring after her.

"Probably Alison's parents with an update." Becky shrugged. "We'd better just leave her alone." But half an

hour later, when Alison still hadn't returned, Becky went looking for her. The barn light was on, so she slipped inside. She heard a voice and stopped. Alison was talking to Shadow!

Becky felt a pang. She hadn't realized Alison confided in Shadow, too. She was about to creep away when she heard her name.

"Becky was right!" Alison was saying. "I should never have taken you on that ride—you could have got swept away in the river or trapped in a mine tunnel. You were so brave, coming to get help, and I'm so glad you're all right!"

Becky heard a soft whinny from Shadow, as if she were answering. Then Alison went on, "And Becky's right about something else, too! I *did* neglect you when we first moved to Horner Creek. I blamed you for everything that was wrong in my life. I'm sorry, Shadow." Alison's voice had a softness that Becky had hardly ever heard before.

"So, what am I going to do with you now? I might have to go back to New York at the end of the summer ..."

There was a long moment of silence. Becky walked the center hall of the barn to Shadow's stall. "I heard," she told Alison. "I guess you've had some news from your parents."

Alison's dark eyes were wet with tears. "I wish they'd just make up their minds!"

Becky came and put her arms around her cousin. "What's happened?"

"Th-they're going to spend the rest of the summer 'giving it another try,' as my mother calls it," said Alison bitterly. "If it works, Mom and I are going to leave Horner Creek and go back to live in New York with Dad."

"Aren't you happy? You never really liked Horner Creek that much."

"I guess so, but I … I liked barrel racing there … and I've got all these new clothes." Alison put her head on Becky's shoulder and sobbed.

Becky knew this was about more than Alison's wardrobe. Poor Alison! "There's lots of barrel racing in the east," she soothed.

"I know that." Alison broke away from Becky's embrace. "But I feel just like poor Shadow. She got shipped east, then shipped west, maybe now shipped east again! Poor horse!" She stroked Shadow's brown and white face. "We've both been treated like ping-pong balls."

"It is too bad," Becky sympathized. She ran her hand down Shadow's shoulder. "She's finally getting used to this new country."

Alison suddenly stepped back and held up both hands. "Wait a minute! I've just had the most brilliant idea. Why should Shadow be sent across the country again? Why can't she stay here, with you?" Her dark eyes flashed. "No, don't stop me—this is the best idea I've had for a long time. You trained Shadow, you looked after her when I was too … too selfish to care about her, and you rode her back from Rainbow Valley to save us all. I heard

you talking to Rob tonight. You wish Shadow was your horse!"

"Alison ... what are you talking about?"

Alison paced the barn floor. "Admit it, you do!"

"Of course I'd love to have Shadow," Becky stammered, "b-but she's your horse. *You* adopted her from the wild. *You* saved her life!"

"That's why I have to give her to you!" Alison stopped pacing and pressed her face against Shadow's cheek again. "I can't take her back to cities and arenas and crowds. She doesn't belong there. She belongs here, at Mustang Mountain."

Becky stared at her. "Alison ..." she began.

"Don't argue, it's settled!" Alison turned and hurried away.

CHAPTER 29

RETURN OF THE HORSES

Alison strode out of the barn. She felt mad and glad and miserable all at once. Such strong emotions upset Shadow. "Still," she told herself, "it's a great idea to give her to Becky, even if it feels terrible." She remembered how hard she'd fought to adopt Shadow in the first place, and how she'd even defied her fierce old grandmother to do it.

The night air was sweet, and stars were starting to come out over the mountain peaks.

Someone else was watching the stars.

Alison walked over and stood beside Chuck at the corral fence. "Hi."

"Oh, hi! It's you. I wondered where you'd gone," Chuck tried to sound surprised. "I mean, I'm glad it's you. I've been wanting to thank you again for saving me ..."

"You're welcome." Alison smiled. She liked Chuck a lot better since Heartbreak Valley. He'd stopped putting on that goofy guy act. Even his hair didn't look so red in the moonlight.

Chuck gave a long, deep sigh. "Can we talk about what happened in the mine the other night? I can't stop thinking about it."

"Neither can I," Alison admitted. "I feel like I started the whole thing with Diablo."

"It wasn't just you." Chuck looked down at her. "I was following him all that first day. He was there, just out of the corner of my eye, leading me on. After what happened to Copper, I knew Thomas was in trouble if he was following that black horse! When I crossed the ridge into Heartbreak Valley, there he was right enough, standing on a high ledge with his mane blowing in the wind." Chuck swallowed hard. "I went after him. He disappeared just as I reached the tunnel. I thought he must be in there, but as soon as I was inside, I realized he had me trapped. If you hadn't come along when you did ..." Chuck gulped again.

"I guess we'll never know what we really saw," Alison murmured. "Diablo kind of seems like a dream already."

Chuck shuddered. "It feels more like a nightmare to me. If I hadn't gone into the river after him ..." His voice was rough. "Copper would still be alive."

"I'm so sorry." Alison put her arm through his. "I lost a horse, once. She didn't die, but my parents sold her

without telling me. Her name was Duchess. I know how much it hurts to lose a horse you love."

They were both quiet for a long time, looking at the stars. Alison tried not to think about Shadow, about leaving her with Becky and going back to New York at the end of the summer. She blinked back tears and leaned on Chuck's shoulder, but a whiff of his shirt made her jump back.

"Have you changed your clothes since we got back?"

"No." Chuck shrugged his broad shoulders. "I've been so caught up thinking about Copper ... I guess they need a good wash, huh?"

"I'll wash them for you," Alison offered. "I'd like to make up for ... for being such a snob about that."

"You've got a deal," Chuck laughed.

He has a nice laugh, Alison thought.

Early the next afternoon, Laurie and Dan came riding through the ranch's gate with a string of horses to loud cheers.

Laurie brought them up to date on the horses' condition at lunch.

"It'll take a couple of weeks for Windy's stone bruise to heal, a month or so more for Agnes to be sound," Laurie said. "Palouse and all the others are fine, and Shadow is superb! I've just had a look at her. That little horse is made of steel."

Alison saw Becky's face break out in a broad smile.

"We're going to have such a good time training her, and Breezy, and Windy when she gets better," she told her mother. "Best of all, Alison wants to leave Shadow at Mustang Mountain if she goes back to New York."

"Even if I don't." Alison shrugged. "She's your horse now."

"Are you sure?" Laurie looked piercingly at her niece.

"Positive." Alison shrugged again. "Chuck's going to help me look for a barrel racing horse," she added. I did the right thing, she thought, seeing the look on Becky's face.

Dan glanced at Chuck. "I was real sorry to hear what happened to Copper," he said. "I'd like to make you an offer. You're welcome to work on the ranch and earn yourself a horse."

"Thanks." Chuck nodded. "I appreciate the offer."

"How about you, Thomas?" Dan said. "I can sure use you around here, too, if you'd like to stay."

"Thank you," Thomas said politely, glancing at Meg. "But Palouse and I will be moving on as soon as Meg leaves on Saturday." He and Meg looked at each other across the table. Their happiness in being together, and their sadness about saying good-bye in a couple of days, hung around them like a cloud.

After lunch Meg and Thomas went for a walk and talked about the ghost horse. "I've been thinking about Diablo." Thomas took Meg's hand. "He couldn't decide whether to save or destroy. I believe it was Alison who made up his mind."

"Maybe," Meg agreed, "but Alison feels guilty. She's afraid she conjured Diablo out of the mist by suggesting you go after him that day she was attacked by the moose. I think the real reason she's giving Shadow to Becky is to make up for all the trouble she's caused."

Thomas shook his head. "It wasn't Alison's fault. According to Slim, Diablo's ghost was haunting that valley long before we came."

"Do you think he's still there?"

"I don't know, but if he is, I don't think he will be a danger to anyone." Thomas smiled at her. "I believe that his spirit is part of the valley now and will be at rest."

Thomas let go of Meg's hand and turned her to face him. "My head's feeling better, but some things are still fuzzy from that time in the cave. Did I ...? Did we ...?"

Meg laughed. "You said I was too young for you," she declared. "You said you were afraid I would change. And you kissed me—don't you remember that?"

She could see a flush creep up Thomas's neck. "You mean, like this?" He leaned forward and brushed her lips with his.

"Something like that." Meg nodded. It wasn't the same kind of kiss at all, but it would do, for now.

"I wish you didn't have to go." Thomas drew in his breath. "But this time, I promise to bury you in e-mails."

"And I'm saving every spare cent to come back," Meg said. "I'll start looking for equine colleges out west ... it's only two and a half years away."

"And meanwhile," she gulped, "you'll be working on

your wild horse refuge. It's a great way to remember Diablo and all the wild horses who used to roam these mountains—and to save the mustangs that are left."

"Chuck will help," Thomas told her. "The wild horse refuge is his idea, too."

Meg nodded, watching his face, so alive with his dreams. Inside she was thinking, How will I live until I see you again? How can I stand to go so far away?

CHAPTER 30

CHUCK'S SURPRISE

The next morning, Alison burst into the boys' bunkhouse waving Chuck's clean clothes.

"Look what I found in the pocket of his jeans!" She dumped the clothes on a bunk and held up something shiny.

Rob and Thomas crowded around to look.

"My watch, thanks." Chuck made a grab for it.

"Not so fast! This is a seven-thousand-dollar watch. Luckily it's waterproof. It survived the washing machine —and the river." She waved the watch over his head. "Chuck McClintock, is this really your watch?"

Thomas made a move toward the bunkhouse door. "Stay here," Alison ordered him. "I have a feeling you know something about Chuck you're not telling."

She held up a badly stained white shirt. "This," she announced, "is a very expensive piece of clothing. Finest Egyptian cotton. And these," she held up a pair of socks, "have the label of an exclusive men's store in New York."

Chuck was grinning until his freckles threatened to fly off his face. "I should have known better than to let you wash my clothes," he said.

Thomas was convulsed with silent laughter. "I guess you'd better confess, *Charles*."

"Yes," Alison said. "What about it, Charles?"

Chuck shrugged. "You tell her, Thomas. I'm too embarrassed."

"Meet Charles Rodney Maxwell McClintock," Thomas said solemnly. "Heir to one of the biggest fortunes in Alberta!"

"I *thought* there was something funny about you." Rob was staring at Chuck. "You're *that* McClintock. Your family owns the Bar Q Ranch. You're rich!"

✳

News that Chuck came from the wealthy McClintock family spread around the ranch like wildfire.

"I feel kind of foolish offering you a job," Dan said that night at dinner.

"No, that's okay," Chuck told him. "I like to pay my own way. That's one of the things that gets me into trouble with my grandfather. He'd buy me any horse I wanted, but he also wants to rule my life in return. I'd still like to take you up on your offer."

Alison stared at him. Her eyebrows rose. "*You* have a bossy grandfather?"

"Tries to run my life," Chuck said sadly. "He's a wicked old skinflint."

"I have a grandmother who is exactly the same!" Alison exclaimed. "She's the one who caused the trouble between my parents ... she tries to rule all our lives!"

"He wants to send me to a college back east to get *polished*," Chuck said. "As if I was a chunk of rock!"

"I know! My grandmother will hate me barrel racing ..." Alison nodded. "She hates everything western, even my western family!"

Meg and Becky shared a surprised glance. "Looks like they're kindred spirits," Meg whispered. "Have you ever seen Alison look so ... so ..."

"Happy," said Becky. "I'm glad Chuck's going to stick around for the summer."

Meg remembered how she had wished that Alison might find something, or someone, to distract her. It looked like Chuck was it. If only I wasn't leaving on Saturday, she thought miserably. The six of us could have so much fun!

Saturday morning, the horses were saddled and bridled, ready to set off down the mountain. They were all going halfway down the trail to see Meg off. Thomas would drive her to the Calgary airport in Rob's red pickup.

While the group waited for Alison to put the finishing

touches on her riding-down-the-trail outfit, Meg and Rob had a private moment. "Looks like you don't have to worry about getting stuck between Becky and Alison anymore," Meg beamed. "Something's happened!"

Rob grinned shyly. "Those two cousins are as thick as thieves since Alison gave Shadow to Becky. I might have trouble getting Becky to spend any time with me."

"Well," Meg said, "maybe if you just came out and told her how you feel once in a while it might help." She was thinking of Thomas.

Rob stared at her. "You're right." He grinned. "I'll talk to her on the way down the mountain and all the way back up the trail to Mustang Mountain."

"*The trail to Mustang Mountain ...*" Meg took a last look at the snow-capped peaks, the green mountain meadows and the trail winding away to the east. "I think those are my favorite words in the world."

ABOUT THE AUTHOR

Sharon Siamon was crazy about two things as a child—books and horses.

Born in Saskatoon, Saskatchewan, Sharon grew up in a farming area of Ontario. She learned to ride by coaxing the farmer's big work horses over to rail fences with apples, then climbing on their backs and riding bareback till they scraped her off under the hawthorn trees that grew along the fence. She wished for a horse of her own, and read every horse book she could find.

Sharon has been writing books ever since for kids who dream of having adventures on horseback, among them, *Gallop for Gold*, and *A Horse for Josie Moon*. The Mustang Mountain adventures began with a wilderness horseback trip through the Rocky Mountains. So far, the books have been translated into Norwegian, German, Finnish and Swedish.

Sharon writes back to all the fans who write to her at her email address: <u>sharon@sharonsiamon.com</u>.

COLLECT ALL THE MUSTANG MOUNTAIN BOOKS!

Mustang Mountain #1: Sky Horse (1-55285-456-6)

Meg would do almost anything to get to Mustang Moutain Ranch—even put up with her snobby friend, Alison. They're going to spend the whole summer with Alison's cousin Becky on a ranch high in the Rocky Mountains. Meg wants a horse so badly. Maybe she'll find a horse on the ranch that will be her special friend. But at the last minute, their trip is delayed and they head into the mountains too late. A sudden storm, an icy road—an adventure begins that will take Meg, Alison and Becky far off the beaten track to a place where cougars, wild mustangs and grizzly bears roam free. To reach Mustang Mountain, they will need every scrap of courage they possess.

Mustang Mountain #2: Fire Horse (1-55285-457-4)

Meg, Alison and Becky find themselves alone at the
Mustang Mountain Ranch in the Rocky Mountains after
an accident puts Becky's mother in the hospital. When
two horses go missing and a cougar is seen prowling
the area, the girls and their friend Henry set out on a
rescue mission. As a forest fire rages around them, they
must depend on their ingenuity and the help of a wild
mustang stallion to save themselves and the horses.

Mustang Mountain #3: Night Horse (1-55285-363-2)

Meg, Alison and Becky return to the Mustang Mountain Ranch high in the Rockies for the summer, where a beautiful mare named Windy is about to give birth to her first foal. It isn't long before a chance meeting with a young rancher lets Meg in on an explosive secret: a bounty hunter has been hired to kill the wild horses that roam the hills. But when Windy escapes from the ranch and into the wilderness, it's up to the girls to protect the mare and the wild stallion, Wildfire. In the long night, who can they trust?

Mustang Mountain #4: Wild Horse (1-55285-413-2)

When Meg, Alison and Becky go to Wyoming to spend their holiday on a ranch, Meg and Becky are thrilled with the promise of riding wild horses. But when Alison refuses to participate and complains about everything, it looks like the entire vacation may be a disaster. Then Alison discovers a wild horse that needs her help. As hope for the sick horse fades, she must conquer her anger and come up with a plan to save it.

Mustang Mountain #5: Rodeo Horse (1-55285-467-1)

As Alison basks in her newly discovered rodeo talents, Becky struggles to train the wild horse Shadow, and find out more about Sam, the mysterious brother of a champion barrel racer. Meanwhile Meg is stuck in New York, longing to join them at the Calgary Stampede. As the Stampede fast approaches, they are all anxious to take part but an accident threatens their plans. Or was it an accident? Together they must overcome their differences to find out the truth.